Pride Publishing books by Bailey Bradford

Single Books
Breaking the Devil
Dark Nights and Headlights
Texas and Tarantulas
Belt Buckles and Cowboy Boots
Something Shattered
Yes, Forever
The Jasper Soul

Southwestern Shifters
Rescued
Relentless
Reckless
Rendered
Resilience
Reverence
Revolution
Revenge
Reluctance
Renounced
Retrograde

Southern Spirits
A Subtle Breeze
When the Dead Speak
All of the Voices
Wait Until Dawn
Aftermath
What Remains
Ascension
Whirlwind

Love in Xxchange
Rory's Last Chance
Miles To Go
Bend
What Matters Most

Ex's and O's
A Bit of Me
A Bit of You
In My Arms Tonight
Where There's a Will
My Heart to Keep

Leopard's Spots
Levi
Oscar
Timothy
Isaiah
Gilbert
Esau
Sullivan
Wesley
Nischal
Justice
Sabin
Cliff

Mossy Glenn Ranch
Chaps and Hope
Ropes and Dreams
Saddles and Memories
Fences and Freedom
Riding and Regrets
Broncs and Bullies
Hay and Heartbreak
Vaqueros and Vigilance

Spotless
Hide
Hunt
Home
Heart

Mystic Tattoos
One Too Many

Valen's Pack
Run with the Moon
Exodus

The Vamp for Me
My Life Without Garlic
Don't Stake My Life on It
Sunshine is Overrated
Don't Drink the Holy Water
The Trouble with Mirrors
That's One Cross Vamp

Calendar Men
Mr. January
Mr. February
Mr. March
Mr. April
Mr. May
Mr. June
Mr. July
Mr. August
Mr September
Mr. October
Mr. November
Mr. December
The 13th Month

Coyote's Call
Off Course
In from the Cold
Blue Moon Rising

Power
Exchange
Submit
Dominate

Hooked on You
In Deep

Intrinsic Values
Artifacts
Antiques
Bygones

City Shifters
Bearly There
Harey Situation

Wild Ones
Destined Prey
Destined Predator
Destined Prize

Fire and Flutter
Dragon Dreams and Fairy Wings
Wyvern Ways and Elven Magic
Griffin Days and Pixie Nights

Triple Threat
Howling for More

Anthologies
What's his Passion?: Unexpected Places
What's his Passion?: Unexpected Moments
Racing Hearts: The Lonely Ones

Intrinsic Values

BYGONES

BAILEY BRADFORD

Bygones
ISBN # 978-1-80250-534-4
©Copyright Bailey Bradford 2023
Cover Art by Claire Siemaszkiewicz ©Copyright May 2023
Interior text design by Claire Siemaszkiewicz
Pride Publishing

Published in 2023 by Pride Publishing, United Kingdom.

BYGONES

Dedication

To everybody who's ever had difficulty in getting through. Hang in there. It gets better.

Chapter One

"So, if you could just stand there against the wall for the photo, Professor Abrams?"

It wasn't really a question. At least, there was no way Jonas could refuse either the young woman's not-really-a-request or her pointing arm, as much as he'd rather turn and leave the building. He ran his hands through his dark-brown hair to settle the curls that tended to form and look more casual than professional. He needed a veneer at the moment.

"Won't take a minute," she assured him, telling him he was hesitating. "Promise it won't hurt!"

He tried to match her professional smile, to show that her small joke had put him at his ease. She used that upspeak intonation that made her sentences not-quite questions. Everyone her age did, or so it seemed to Jonas, teaching them. Students at his prior college in Dallas had been fans of that pattern too. It was even catching, something he had to guard against for fear of seeming a try-hard, this millennial trying to be a zoomer.

"Perfect." She said this more briskly and brightly, doling out the word of praise like a cookie when he stood against the wall with its lines that marked out heights. Another blonde clicked the camera, taking his photograph, and although the lights weren't hot, Jonas wanted to wipe his forehead. *And wouldn't that just make me look ill at ease?*

"Now turn your face to the side?" And they were back to the rising intonation.

"A real mug shot," he couldn't help saying.

Her perfunctory laugh showed he was far from the first to make that remark. He'd bet he was the one who hated having his picture taken the most, though. Well, they could hardly use the one from the history faculty page on San Antonio's Laurel Heights University website. As an adjunct professor in the history department, despite his master's in art history and PhD in American history, not even his name was listed.

A fellow adjunct had raged that the university was wary of including them on anything official because it might make them look like legitimate faculty members, not just paid-per-semester hired guns, which could give them leverage for getting onto the tenure track. It was the same at most institutions these days, and Jonas counted himself lucky he had his work for Intrinsic Values antiques store, sourcing items for clients, and working at the store itself, to make up his salary.

"Hm…maybe to the other side? Perfect." His tormentor gave him another automatic word of praise for obeying and signaled to her henchwoman to take his photo again. She raised her eyebrows to the photographer to ask if it looked okay. When she received an A-okay sign back, she nodded at Jonas. "So, if you're ready, and would like to go through for a few questions…?" She gestured at a smaller room.

And now he really wanted to turn tail and run. *A few questions* was the polite way they'd put it before, back in Dallas, their name for the repeated rounds of inquiries about the same thing put by different people. *Interlocutors?* No, that was more the panel when he'd defended his thesis. *Interviewers? Interrogators?* Whatever, they'd included his department head, the assistant dean, the welfare officers…the police. Then Human Resources, with their offer he couldn't refuse and didn't want to refuse, by then, for all he was innocent.

After all that, this. Why was he here? He'd tried to keep the lowest possible profile. He'd even left teaching for a while, before making his tentative way back in. But oh, how he'd missed it, missed engaging with history, missed reading and researching and even the smell of libraries and books. If only that was enough, if the quality of his work and his thoughts on the existing courses spoke for themselves. But they didn't, and certainly wouldn't get his ideas for new courses, ones he'd be excited to develop and teach, off the drawing board.

He knew how the game was played, that if he wanted to get on, or get in, he had to make an effort, to become more a part of things. So when the department had needed someone for this and the associate and assistant professors had looked his way, his vague smile and nod had been taken as him volunteering.

He took off his black-framed glasses, breathed on them, wiped them with a cloth and put them back on, giving a sly pat to blot his forehead as he did so. And the interview hadn't even started yet. Well, putting himself out there made him break out into a sweat.

"You know what we do here at *Academically Speaking*?"

That was the name of the radio show he was here at the Laurel Heights campus media building to take part in. He nodded at the girl, Ainsley's, question, taking a seat at her direction at the small console in front of the equipment.

"Great name!" praised another guest, hurrying in and taking the remaining empty chair on the other side of the host. He looked to be a little younger than Jonas' early thirties but a lot more energetic. "The Hill's station rocks! Well, all the media facilities do. And I love how seriously you take the content you produce, with the professional yet quirky photos and a summary of the day's highlights for your social media. And this program's an arts versus science thing, right?"

He swept a flop of dark-blond hair from his blue eyes that crinkled at the corners with his smile. Jonas couldn't help staring—discreetly, he hoped. Trying to see if the man was wearing makeup, for the photographs, and to place his accent meant Jonas tuned out a little from proceedings as they got underway, then he snapped to when Ainsley pointed at him to speak.

"I'm Jonas Abrams, and I'm in the history department teaching Introduction to History Studies," he said, trying to put a smile in his voice, as everything he'd looked up about speaking on the radio had advised.

Ainsley's bulging-eyed nod and the quick hand-roll gesture had him dredging for more. "I recently taught Introductory History of Art too, all to freshmen, and

I'm hopefully getting students enthusiastic about history." He added a physical smile to compensate for how lame that sounded. A private person—more so these days—he wasn't about to give out further personal details. He slid the department prospectus from his briefcase so he could describe any or each of the courses they offered, should he need to.

"And with us today we also have…" Giving up on Jonas, their talk show host cued the other guy in.

Professor Bruce was Australian, Jonas learned, and a lot bouncier and bubblier than Jonas would ever be.

"My big dream in teaching is to make mathematics accessible to all Heights students, no matter their background or major," Professor Bruce enthused.

"Oh, how?" their host asked, sounding genuinely interested.

"Well, for starters, making mathematics relevant to other disciplines like biology, economics, physics or engineering," the professor continued. "Putting the emphasis on mathematical concepts and their underlying ideas, not techniques and details."

Adjectives such as *interactive* and *enjoyable* bounced loose from his speech, and Jonas leaned over to a small table to help himself to water from a jug, hoping the noise of pouring it into a plastic cup wasn't audible. He needed the water before he launched into the speech he'd prepared. This radio program was all about justifying the teaching of the subjects in question, both the arts and science, and Jonas had a lot to say about the vital importance of history, and about learning from the past to understand the present.

"History gives us a better understanding of the world," he began when cued in.

"Erm, no disrespect," Professor Bruce interrupted, "but I'd say mathematics gives us a better understanding...of the universe! You ask me, history is learning a dry and dusty string of dates and facts, like 776, the first Olympic Games, or 1770, Captain Cook arrives in Australia or 1917, the Russian Revolution." He paused. "Hey, anyone else think that's a load of sh...sevens?"

"Yes!" Ainsley replied, with a tiny giggle.

"It's more than memorizing numbers. I think you're confusing history with mathematics," Jonas couldn't help replying.

"Ooh!" His opponent feigned being wounded, which got a laugh from their host and a studio technician. "And the problem with these dry facts is that a lot turn out to be wrong, and a lot we're bloody ashamed of and try to ignore or lie about!"

"Like what?" Jonas snapped, stung.

"Like... Oh let's see. You're an expert in American history, you said? Well, like who discovered America? It wasn't exactly Columbus, was it, although every schoolkid was taught that? He was one of a long line of explorers, and he didn't even get the place named after him!"

He drawled the word 'after' as '*aaaaftah*' and paused for the laugh. "What he did do, though, was destroy old civilizations and enslave and kill a few million Red and Brown people along the way, right? Correct me if I'm wrong, Prof, but didn't he torture and mutilate indigenous populations while stealing millions of acres of their land?"

This didn't get laughs, of course, but was met by indrawn breaths from the production crew. Ainsley recovered quickly. "You're talking about a figure seen as a national hero there, Professor Bruce," she said. "A founding father of America, you know?"

"Yeah. He was even proposed for sainthood at one point," Bruce replied, rolling his eyes.

"Professor Abrams?" Ainsley prompted, bugging out her eyes at him again.

"Yes, well, while none of what you mentioned can or should be condoned," Jonas started, "let's also consider that the Old World also brought to the Americas new concepts and commodities, such as methods of farming or business or governance, or goods such as textiles—"

"Ah, sorry." Bruce held up his hands in mock surrender. "I guess I spoke too soon when I said ignore or lie about. I should have said ignore, lie about or find excuses for!"

That got a whistle of appreciation, and the Australian flashed them all a gleaming grin. "Now can I tell you what's so fantastic about mathematics?" he asked, leaning forward into the mic.

* * * *

"Well, that was really informative!" Ainsley gushed after Professor Bruce's infomercial on the skills that studying math developed in a person, and how any or all of them, from problem-solving to data analysis, led to glittering careers and a better life. "Now, let's take a few calls about what we've heard or any thoughts it might have sparked? And remember we don't go out just to the Heights campus but to the surrounding area, so we never know who's listening!"

Jonas' abrupt jerk spilled his water, and he rammed his arm down over the trickle for his sleeve to catch it. There was no way he could leave, right now, was there?

"And the first caller is for —"

"Professor Bruce! Professor Bruce, will you marry me?" begged the girl on the other end of the phone line, interrupting Ainsley and generating more laughter in the studio. "Not just because you called out Columbus' genocide of indigenous peoples and environmental destruction but —"

Ainsley cut her off before she went into detail, and Bruce deflected her offer, and that of the next caller along the same lines.

"A caller for Professor Abrams," Ainsley said, a second before a click was heard, signaling a hang-up. "Oh."

Jonas took in a deep breath, letting it out slowly. He didn't want to speak to anyone, particularly, but didn't like the feeling this gave him, either. Thankfully the question-and-answer section wasn't long, and he was out of there as soon as he'd thanked the host and team, not staying for any post-match analysis.

"Professor Abrams, wait up!" a voice called behind him as soon as he'd reached the path outside the media building.

Too polite to pretend he hadn't heard, Jonas turned to see Bruce bounding down the steps.

"Jonas, right? Wayne." He grinned. "I know, I know. Wayne Bruce. And Bruce, for an Aussie?" His smile turned self-deprecating, and he stuck out a hand that Jonas had no option other than to shake. With his free hand, Wayne Bruce pushed at his thatch of hair. "Listen, sorry about all that."

"All that?" Repeating the last two words back using the dreaded upspeak was a technique Jonas often employed. It was useful. He slid his hand free.

"The ding-dong back there." Bruce jerked his head at the building and his squint had those lines around his eyes fanning out. It looked practiced. "Think I blindsided you a bit, eh?"

"Blindsided? *Broad*sided, you mean." As in, he'd let Jonas have both barrels.

"Sorry, mate. Things you do for ratings, right? Oh, not just the program's, although they do take their stuff seriously, with the media and marketing students puffing it up beforehand and the creative writing and journo students writing it up after for course projects or whatever. Nah, you know how it is, how you have to stir things up, make a bit of a name for yourself, when you're the low man on the totem pole?"

So all that discomfort, that provocation was for show? "Pity you don't know more history." Jonas glared through his glasses. "Then you'd know that in First Nations culture, the lowest figures on the totem pole are often considered the *most* prestigious. Think about it—the designs on the bottom six feet are the ones that will be seen at eye level, so the master carver works on the lower end."

"Strewth, no need to get all snooty about things, mate." Bruce took a step back. "Was gonna ask you out for a drink, get to know you, you know? It's my first semester here at the biggest small university in Texas— isn't that the slogan?

"Best," Jonas answered. "Best small university in Texas."

"Yeah…and is it true that everything's bigger in Texas?" Bruce let his gaze travel up and down Jonas.

"Wouldn't know. Thanks but no thanks. And I think you'll fit in well here." Jonas tried a version of Bruce's beaming smile and walked away.

He had no intention of getting involved with any colleague. *Been there, done that, and got trampled on in his rush to get ahead. Ben couldn't get away from me quick enough when the whole thing went down, eager to toe the department line.* Bruce was cut from that cloth. Jonas didn't play in that pool any longer. He scratched his itches elsewhere, far from the ivory tower, or even the white-collar world.

His fast pace knocked his briefcase against his leg and made him think about its contents, the minor and possibly major in museum studies he was hoping to create and that he was on his way to discuss. Museum studies didn't seem a big thing in this city, not even at the other colleges, but Jonas believed the possibilities, the joy of experiential learning about artifacts could be communicated. He was still excited about it.

Maybe things — and the future — were fine here?

But Jonas was a historian — he knew the past had long shadows. And so he quickened his pace and rolled his shoulders, trying to shrug them off.

Chapter Two

"Them good ol' boys, Whiskey and Rye,' Starmer sang, or tried to, coming into Jake's Diner as Field Ranger Gabe Ryland and his partner, Chip Daniels, were leaving.

Chip scowled. "Remind me to get ya a bucket there, Starman. It's the only way you'll ever carry a tune."

"Good one, y'all." Rye ran his fingers through his straw-blond hair, raking it back behind his ears before pulling on his buff-colored western hat, which he tipped in salute to Chip's comeback.

He stood back to let the three other Company F members enter Jake's, thinking as he had before that a group of Rangers were more obviously Rangers than one alone. A lot of Texans, even here in Waco, wore western hats and boots, and a few favored bolo ties, like Rye did, but a bunch of tall, broad guys in the khaki or gray pants and double belt was a dead giveaway. Not that Rye would try to hide who he was or what he did. He was damn proud to be a Ranger.

Them using this diner was another clue. Just off the Texas Ranger Trail, where the Waco HQ stood, it was a traditional hangout for those coming off shift, like Starmer and Sena, and those going on the graveyard shift, like him and Chip. He shot a glance at his partner's hard face. Something was off.

"The Starman's just being his usual asshole self." Rye jerked his chin back at the diner. "Making his same old fuckin' — "

"Cheesy jokes that weren't even funny the first time around," Chip finished. He blew out a breath. "No. I know. It's just I don't like surveillance detail, you know?"

Yeah. Rye did know. It felt kinda like being back on patrol, as if they were once again Texas Highway Patrol officers, not yet Rangers. Five years older than Rye's early thirties, Chip had been in the ranks longer than Rye had before making it through and getting duty-assigned here. Rye had wondered recently if Chip was contemplating a station transfer. He couldn't have said why. Just a feeling something was on his partner's mind.

He nodded. "Well, we're all Department of Public Safety."

"And Rangers are supposed to be its major criminal investigative agency. Can't say it feels like we're investigating a major crime or conducting a special investigation sat on our fuckin' asses tailing a suspect," Chip complained, getting into the car then slamming the door.

"Can't all be riot suppression or fugitive apprehension," Rye pointed out. It didn't matter — every part of their duties made a difference. "What, you'd prefer y'all investigate some cattle rustling?"

That didn't get a smile from Charles 'Chip' Daniels this evening. "What's with the bug up your ass? Everything okay at home?"

Chip was silent so long that Rye didn't think he was going to answer, but then he gave a half-shrug. "Lina ain't too happy being left all by herself at nights."

That aspect of their job, their life, wasn't something Rye couldn't say he understood. He'd never had a partner, in that meaning of the word. Relationships, sure, some longer than others, and a couple less casual than others. His lips curled into a smile thinking of Dan, his 'hub' of almost a year. Dan had come up with that term, and it wasn't anything to do with husband. *Hookup buddy.*

Jesus, just thinking of some of the stuff they'd gotten up to and the places they'd done it had Rye's fuckin' balls tightening and him shifting in his seat. How to describe that sort of relationship, or his handling of his sexuality? *Not flaunting it*, was the best he'd come up with. He would never deny who he was but couldn't see himself bringing a guy into Jake's to say *howdy y'all* to the other Field Rangers over a chicken-fried steak breakfast, or to one of Sena's backyard cook-outs for beers and burgers…as much as he might want to. That pang, coming from nowhere, took him by surprise, and Rye dragged himself into the present, the here and now, to focus.

"Sorry about Lina," he muttered, switching on the equipment to get their handover from the current team who were finishing the mobile surveillance of their target. "Let's see what Luis 'The Animal' Amaral's been up to since we last checked, huh?"

The usual big fat fuckin' nothing seemed to be the answer, for all their mark was a rumored member of the Camargo cartel, a known DTO, or drug trafficking organization, running wholesale distribution networks from South America and Mexico inward. Rye had attended the briefings on the smuggling of cocaine and methamphetamine shipments over the South Texas border area, the temporary storing in stash houses around there then the transportation of the drug shipments to other distribution centers in Texas.

Chip slid the vehicle into position for them to take over the surveillance of Amaral's property without them being visible, but they'd barely settled in, watching the gates, before they opened and Amaral's heavily modified Lexus GX tore out.

"Shit!" Rye sat straight and stared through the night-vision binoculars. "That's him. Get after him, Chip! Chip?"

Nodding, Chip started the engine for them to tail the Lexus at a safe distance. Rye frowned, running through a mental list of possible locations Amaral could be heading for. What was out here? No clubs or bars beyond a dive of a roadhouse, and The Animal continued past where he should have turned off for that. That special kind of tension, like an extra sense, an alert, gripped Rye. Something was happening.

"I don't fucking believe it." Raising his head from the map, Rye whistled through his teeth. "The airfield. That's got to be where he's heading, There's nothing else around here."

Small aircraft landed and took off from the private local field all the time. There was no control tower, just a small single strip and a lone hangar. Ideal for what Amaral and his men were suspected of

"See?" Rye hissed in triumph when the Lexus turned onto the property, making for the far end. Its headlights showed it wasn't the only vehicle there, but the sweep of the beam was too fast and the cars too distant to observe more. "We need those license plates." And if they could fuckin' get photos of the drivers...

"We'll stand out. Set up an observation point in the woods to the south?" Chip pointed.

"The hell. Get as close as y'all can," Rye argued. "You were bitching about sitting on your ass with this night after night—maybe we can crack it wide open."

"And if a plane approaches, you gonna shoot it out of the fuckin' sky?" Chip mocked.

"Shit, Chip!" Rye glared at him. "We're on surveillance, so let's do the job we got given and get as much intel as we can, right?"

Chip didn't reply but parked with the airfield in sight, and where their vehicle could be hidden. "And now?"

"Now you go around the perimeter from the left. I'm gonna go right. Meet you down the back." Rye was out of the car before Chip could argue. His partner's hesitation irritated him. Lina must have been doing a number on him. They'd been married long enough that she knew the score...or was that the problem, that they'd been married long enough and the score was still the same...and she wanted a higher one, or a completely different one?

Shit, he should drag Chip out for a beer at MacLaren's sooner rather than later, get him to talk about stuff. Rye was a loner, someone who'd grown up quick at the age of seventeen when their parents' road traffic accident death had left him the only family to his younger sister. He'd juggled school with work, making sure he brought in enough money to pay rent and put food on the table, and while the only way he knew was to rely on himself and no one else, it seemed Chip needed to share? Only…not right now.

"Go," he urged, checking his flashlight and striding off before Chip could argue more. Hell, it wasn't like Rye was planning on storming in—just a quick sweep of the location, gleaning all the details of vehicles and active participants inside he could while Chip did the same on the other side. A two-pronged attack should result in something.

Rye checked his Sig and backup gun, making sure to keep to the darkness as he moved. The fence around the property was poorly maintained, with lots of gaps in it, easy to squeeze through. This barely classed as infiltration. The weak random lights fixed high here and there turned the grounds into a patchwork of shadows and shade, pitch-black to dusky gray. Rye made himself part of it, careful to produce as little sound as possible. If Chip was doing the same, making a wide sweep from the other side, Rye couldn't hear or see him.

He should have been using his flashlight to check the ground in front of him more thoroughly, but falsely confident at the silence and emptiness, he wasn't—and stepped onto something plastic. Thick plastic, by the feel, an old bag or wrapping, and he froze at the snap and rustle, then cursed under his breath when there was no way he could get his foot off it without it making more goddamn noise. He held his breath as he raised his foot, scanning all around. He hoped he was too far away from the hangar for the sound to register

Staring hard at the hangar building, he saw darker shadows, thick squares on the ground around it, and followed them upward to what made them—small sheds or huts. *Interesting.* He'd thought the only structure on the premises was the hangar and assumed any kind of office or admin desk or counter would be part of it. *So what are these?*

They looked new, temporary, and the vehicles parked, including The Animal's, were situated closer to one than the other, so that was the one Rye chose to sneak up behind. He didn't think it a good fuckin' idea to peek in at the window, but pressed his ear just under it, against the metal wall, to listen. *Shit.* Why couldn't it be an older building with an ill-fitting window or one with a crack? Should he take a quick look?

Three men. All Hispanic, ran his mental notes after a minute's eavesdropping. *Impossible to say if one is Amaral, although high possibility given his vehicle is here.*

"Angel?" he caught, though he missed the question asked.

Angel? Rye checked that name against the ones he knew to be involved. Could they mean Miguel Angelo Garcia Moreno? His nickname was believed to be *Mulatto*, but...

"Fuentes?" the same voice asked, his tone asking for confirmation.

Fuentes? Rye didn't know that name either and didn't have time to ponder on it...because that low, dull humming sound above and getting louder was a plane approaching the airstrip, and he wasn't the only one to hear it. A cell phone rang inside the hut, someone spoke into it and quick exchanges flew from one person to another. The tone...angry? Surprised? Things weren't going to plan?

Whatever, Rye had to act. He took a deep breath and let it out, moving stealthily around the side of the hut and got near to the front just in time to see Chip walking right on up the door. What? *No!* Rye didn't know if he cried out the word or if it just burst inside his head. Oh no, that burst would be the door opening and two men pouring out.

Chip called out, his tone placating, as was his head shake and his palms-up *what could I do?* gesture. Rye didn't know what he said—Chip didn't get out more than a word before a shot rang out and he dropped to the ground. The two men bent briefly over him then checked the path to the cars and in a flurry of movement, the hut emptied, people flowing to their vehicles that sped off in a squeal of sound and blur of motion. It took seconds, time speeding like tape in fast forward...until it stopped, until everything stopped and all that was left was Charles 'Chip' Daniels, lying on the dark ground.

A hundred questions trying to form in his horrified, disbelieving brain, Rye raced to his partner. He dropped to his knees and got an arm under Chip's shoulders to raise them, bring him into a sit. But his partner remained motionless, a dead weight. "Chip?" Rye cried. "The hell?"

Chip didn't answer. Couldn't, any more than he could move. He was dead, the gunshot wound that had torn his chest open still gushing. The louder humming above quieted then faded...because the plane didn't land. It turned a tight half-circle in the air and was gone.

Like Chip. "No! You can't..." Rye choked. Droplets of liquid ran down his face and for a half second, he thought he was sweating, despite the cool night air, until he realized the drops were tears. He hadn't known he was crying and scrubbed the liquid from his eyes in a jerk.

And stupidly, despite all the things he should be puzzling out, like *what the fuck happened?* and *Chip, what the hell were y'all doing?* all that came to him were more words from that song Starmer enjoyed baiting them with. It was a line that came after the part he liked to chant about them good ol' boys, Whiskey and Rye, singing—

This'll be the day that I die.

Rye clutched Chip's lifeless body harder.

Chapter Three

That was great!!! You were great!!!

Jonas stopped in the street and read the text message from Aldric Beamer, the other and younger assistant at Elliot Douglas' Intrinsic Value antiques store. The number of exclamation points and smiling face emojis had *him* smiling too, even though he was still wincing at how much of a fiasco the campus radio show had been. Jonas couldn't really agree with either statement Aldric had sent. He appreciated his co-worker's sentiments, although he doubted Aldric could really mean what he'd texted.

Well, Aldric had promised to listen to Jonas' five minutes of fame — or ignominy — and had kept his word. He always did. For someone so shy and unsure, Aldric was determined and not a pushover. He'd never let his partner Darrell, a much bigger, broader, bolder guy and a SAPD cop in addition, have the last word, let alone boss him around.

Working at the Pearl District store under Elliot had done Aldric a power of good, increasing his self-confidence and self-esteem. And it was how he'd met Darrell, now Sergeant Williams. Just like Elliot had met his partner, a Scotland Yard detective, no less, through working there. It was an unusual place, in many ways.

Trent, their new part-time helper, had begun dating one of the servers from the restaurant opposite the store, leading Andrew, Elliot's other half, to comment that Intrinsic Value specialized in romance as much as it did antiques. Jonas didn't quite feel that was accurate either. If so, wouldn't there be someone for him? The buzz of another message from the phone he still held in his hand made him jump and shake off those self-pitying thoughts. A message from Darrell?

Heard some and you did well. Other guy was a jerk.

Well, Jonas couldn't disagree there. He was about to reply, to send a thanks to both of them, when on impulse he pressed the Call icon under Darrell's name.

"Hi, Jonas." Darrell sounded surprised when he answered. "Everything okay?"

Not really. Just made a fool of myself and not only have I a meeting with members of the department I made look foolish, but I need to try to get something from them. Could he say that? He wasn't known for baring his soul.

"I— Did I...? What is it Drew says, make a bit of a tit of myself?" He wasn't known for using slang either, but there were several sides to him, the darker ones of which the Intrinsic Value crew had no idea about. Jonas worked hard to compartmentalize and keep things that way.

The snort over the line was Darrell fighting a laugh. "That jerk used you to score points." Darrell didn't beat about the bush. "You can't be blamed for him having an agenda."

"No...but I had one too." Why was he calling this man? Jonas moved out of the way of pedestrians and tried to understand why he'd wanted to speak to Darrell.

"You did?" Darrell sounded skeptical then muffled—he must have covered the phone to speak to someone near him.

"I'm interrupting." Jonas couldn't exactly decipher the background noises but guessed Darrell was at work. "Sorry. I'll—"

"You're fine. Go on."

Jonas raised an eyebrow at the authority in Darrell's tone. Sure, he was a law enforcement officer, trained to give orders that the public follow, but Jonas had long felt there was something more innate to the man's need to take charge...to have his *partner* obey his commands. It took one to know one, as they said. And from what Jonas had observed of their interactions, the smaller, gentler Aldric would push at every one of the boundaries set. How did Darrell feel about that?

"Jonas?" Darrell prompted, a little more forcefully.

"Sorry. Thank you." He had to stop speculating on his friends' sex life, wondering about Aldric's occasional hickeys and why he sometimes winced on sitting. "Yes, I had an ulterior motive, but I don't suppose for one minute I accomplished it. I think I mentioned, or it's obvious, that I was trying to get into the good books of my superiors, people who are my de-facto employers at the college. People I have to go to right now if not exactly on bended knee, but something akin to it. The people I was *trying* to please..."

"And you think you didn't please them. Made the department look bad." And Darrell went right to the point again.

But Jonas knew why he'd called Darrell. He'd been through something similar in the SAPD. Darrell had solved a case above his pay grade and rank when no one else would listen to him. He'd come out as gay and taken a position as an LGBT liaison, and as part of that he'd written a report detailing where the institution could do better in serving the LGBT community *and* accommodating its LGBT officers and staff. Then, after that, he'd asked for the promotion that had been vaguely talked about...and got it.

"How did you get your department to do what you wanted?" Jonas blurted out.

Darrell laughed and Jonas could just picture him, tall, broad-shouldered, his hazel eyes crinkled at the corners.

"Jonas, you've never met my father, but you probably know that I was raised by a no-nonsense straight shooter. He's known as Chief. I mean, known *everywhere* as that. My brothers and I call him that. He marches in, stands tall, stares everybody down and lays out his demands. And he gets them! And people respect him for that, and because he's the real deal. Because he's shown all his life that he walks the walk, that he can do what he says he can do, that there's no BS. I don't agree with...everything about him, every opinion he has..."

Jonas knew some of the story, of Silver Star Medal-decorated Jack Williams' refusal to accept his son's sexual orientation.

"But I sure as hell respect his abilities and his belief in them and the way he communicates that," Darrell finished.

Darrell gave off a lower-key but no less firm sense of self, and it was obviously something his fellow law enforcement officials responded to. Did Jonas convey that conviction? Could he?

"But let's think about this from another angle," Darrell said, cutting that chain of thoughts off. *Ah.* Jonas hoped it wasn't because Darrell thought he had no hope of achieving that. "How many of these people you're talking about do you think listen to that station, that program, live? Or would have made an effort to, today?"

"A couple, perhaps?" Jonas replied, thinking back to the staff meeting when it had been discussed. "And maybe not live, but they might catch it later."

"So if there's a buzz about it, some hype, like that Aussie jerk wanted to start, that's maybe only building now? It won't be so loud until the station does its round-up of the day's highlights, later, when they'll probably emphasize it? So you should have a window of time right now. My advice is to use it."

"Thanks. Darrell, thank you." Jonas meant it. That was why he'd called him. Darrell Williams lived in the real world, not that of history and art and bygones. He'd just said his goodbyes when Aldric texted again.

And break a leg for later. Or now!

Now. Right. Jonas put his cell away and wiped his hands where they had sweated a little on the phone and the handle of his briefcase. He should be nearly there — did he have the right place? If it weren't for the smell of coffee and hiss of the espresso machines, he'd have thought this was a trendy bar. "Trendy coffee shop," he murmured, letting the caffeine-infused air charge him, pep him up for his meeting. For his chat about his new course ideas.

The décor startled him a little. The bare stone and brick wall place looked Victorian, with plush buttoned-leather seating and decorative tin molding. It was, however, packed to the rafters with metal tubes and cogs and hissing and clanking machinery. *Surely that can't all be for making coffee and steaming milk?* The vintage machine for roasting coffee, standing proud behind the counter, was enormous, drawing the eye, and Jonas stood and stared.

"Steampunk." A passing waiter took pity on Jonas' obviously confused face and gestured at the room.

"Ah." Enlightened, feeling old, Jonas spied his history and history of art colleagues and a couple of other members of the college in a booth at the back. Why weren't they having this meeting in a meeting room in the department or even in the faculty lounge instead of a place that was all copper and brass and wood and metal? The rapt face of Associate Professor Richard Meyer, the art and art history program director, led Jonas to think he'd picked the venue…because he wanted an excuse to see it.

"All the *meubles* are handmade!" Richard said as Jonas joined them. It wasn't a greeting—he was reading from the leaflet on the table to Cathy, the associate professor who more or less ran the history department.

"It's…eye-catching, yes," Jonas said, for something to say, sliding into a seat. The place being practically empty meant he could see the décor, at any rate. Oh, so maybe it wasn't that bad an idea to hold a meeting here. It was probably more private than the department.

Confronted with a page-long list of coffees, he found he wanted some of the herbal tea Elliot made in Intrinsic Value, with their scents that perfumed the store and added to the notes of cedarwood and lavender Jonas associated with the place. He settled for a cup of the café's blend of the week, taking it black. When it came, it was strong, sending a rush through him.

"So, turning to the idea for a new minor elective, to trial before it becomes a major," he began, at the first gap in the small talk. His mealy-mouthed words, the lack of agency in them, struck him. *No. Stand tall. No BS.* "My idea, I mean, that I'd—*I'll*—trial for a half semester, before directing it as a major."

He tried to ignore the indrawn breaths and shared looks around the table as he launched into his speech about how the college should offer museum studies, from the standpoint of how to empirically interpret, preserve and display works of art and historical artifacts. He emphasized the practical aspect not to tread on any history of art toes.

"Professor Abrams, you came to us as a cover teacher," Cathy began.

"And alongside museum studies, we could structure curatorial studies," Jonas continued, taking more files from his briefcase. "I believe we should teach the understanding and knowledge required to follow a rewarding career as an independent curator or to work within a related sector. San Antonio is well provisioned with museums, yet no other higher education institution in the city offers such a course."

He hated the silence that followed his words. It took him back to the panel he'd faced when he'd presented his PhD thesis, and how his studies had been wrapped up in a hurry with him leaving suddenly. The defense of his work had been a formality, the degree conferred just like that.

"How…?" Cathy trailed off in an exhaled breath and head shake.

She'd probably been going to say *interesting* or *novel* or some other empty adjective, but Jonas pretended it was a question.

"I see it as an opportunity for inviting artists or designers or different speakers from industry to come in to share their knowledge and viewpoints. That would be extremely engaging." He finished his coffee and hated that the cup made a clatter when he placed it down. "This could be an MA, for students with a first degree in fine art or design or art history or history, or could be offered to professionals in the field wanting to develop their career and attain specialist knowledge." And he was back to hypothetical, passive language again.

"Look, I could teach a summer course. An extra credit course," he burst out. "Something that forms more links with local art museums and teaches students to engage with objects and artworks, so they rethink American history, as well as obtain understanding of a functioning museum. They'd work with curators and staff—"

"We do want a museum studies course."

Jonas didn't think he knew the middle-aged man who'd thankfully stopped him but he could have kissed him in the rush of relief that coursed through him.

"But no point trying to run before we can walk. All that 'inviting guest stars'…" The man paused for the murmurs of agreement to die down. "Yes, students can think critically about museums, and so on, but the course content has to be centered on knowledge for successful museum internships and graduate work and the focus needs to be on practical skills in museum management, educational programming and, of course, grant writing."

Jonas remembered who the man was—from the budget and research office. The man's words registered. "That...sounds familiar. Art, history and culture meet business."

"Uh-huh." The man sat forward. "Now, we put out feelers about this..."

"We have to, part of procurement," added another bean counter at his side.

"And we made contact with Dr. Ben Nash," Professor Meyer said.

Jonas jerked, and his chair made a teeth-on-edge scrape.

"Oh, you know him?" Meyer asked. "He's in Dallas."

"Yes. I worked with him." Jonas addressed his reply to his pile of paperwork, on the table.

"So you know his background?" Cathy added.

That and more. Knew how he thought, lived, fucked...and how he scurried away like a rat from the sinking ship that Jonas Abrams had become when charges were leveled against him.

Jonas stood and grabbed at his papers, shoving them into his briefcase. "You've heard all I have to say," he said, trying to keep his voice level. "So, if you'll excuse me?" He looked around the table and wished he had something more profound or even witty to add but didn't. Pasting on a tight smile, he walked out.

He'd tried. He'd— He wouldn't think about it. The machine behind the counter gushed out a billow of steam as he passed, and he nodded. Yes, he needed to let off steam, but not as Jonas, the easily crushed mild-mannered historian. He needed to spend time as someone else, who liked very different bars and places to this, places where he could chase the adrenaline rush of gambling and of a hookup.

Yes, a meaningless fuck…

Chapter Four

Rye stumbled out of Lieutenant LeGrande's office the next day, still in shock, his mind struggling to process and make sense of what had happened at the airfield. With his hat under his arm, he leaned against the wall and, when he could focus, looked around. He'd never been to the lieutenant's office before, or to this section of the Ranger HQ on the Texas Ranger Trail compound.

"Never been fuckin' questioned like that before either," he muttered. They'd recorded him, using both audio and video equipment. That had surprised him. Sure, he'd known he'd be taken through the series of events that had ended with Chip dead. Taken through it officially, step by step, moment by moment. And that was better than having his fellow Rangers fire questions at him and almost shake him for answers when he had no coherent ones to give.

So yeah, he'd known that, but what he hadn't known, or guessed, was how the officials would not just conduct but shape things, like they already had the outline mapped out and wanted the details filled in, with some color and shading added. They'd returned to the same points over and over. It almost felt like they were putting words in his goddamn mouth. He'd make sure he read the official statement from first capital letter to final period before he signed it.

"Gabe." Bruno, one of the few people to call him by his given name, came out of the office after him. He looked up and down the corridor and, even though it was empty, lowered his voice. "I bought you some time back there."

"Yeah."

Bruno worked in admin and had quoted rules and regs to the brass, preventing them from printing out Rye's statement and him signing it before he left their office. Rye had seen the medic, both last night to check for physical injuries, and this morning, to see if he were psychologically fit to withstand questioning. He was.

"And what I said is correct, you have the right to decide if you need trauma or bereavement counseling or support, either workplace or from your healthcare provider. And you don't have to make that decision right away." Bruno took a step nearer.

They'd fucked a few times, a few months back, more or less on the downlow and it hadn't gone anywhere. "*It's never a good idea to fuck where you work,*" Bruno had said.

"*Thought it was 'shit where you eat',*" Rye recalled replying and, in bed post-fuck with a beer, that had seemed real funny.

But now Rye wished they were close, so that he felt someone from the organization was on his side or could at least tell him what was going on. He frowned. That was a wrong kind of thought, wasn't it? Did it even make sense when he was in the goddamn organization himself?

All Rye knew was he didn't like the way things were shaping. No, *being* shaped. Could he ask Bruno about it? Maybe talk to him about it, and get his help to absorb what had happened, because he still couldn't believe his partner Chip, Charles Emory Daniels, was dead from one minute to the next. "Hell, one second to the fuckin' next," he said through gritted teeth.

"What?" Bruno asked.

"I...nothing." Rye raked through his hair and put his hat on.

"Seems a stupid question, but you doing okay?" Bruno asked. "Holding up?"

"Yeah?" Rye replied after a pause.

Bruno gave a half-laugh. "And if I were a Ranger, I'd slap you on the shoulder and say *attaboy* or *good man*. I'm not a Ranger though, so I'm saying, do what it takes to get through this, okay?"

Rye shrugged.

"I'm not a Ranger...but I do hear the station gossip." Bruno turned to go, deliberately stepping nearer as he did. "And what people are saying is you left your partner unprotected when you left your position and raced from the scene. No, not like you were running for cover—" He correctly interpreted Rye's start.

"Better fucking not be," Rye growled, fists clenched. "Any man here thinks I'm a coward can tell me to my goddamn face. And then they'll be sorry." He tried to calm down. "Apart from anything else, my record speaks for me."

Bruno shook his head. "As in, you went charging off lone wolf-style on a hunch."

"I *what*?"

"And left Daniels behind and, well. The rest happened." Bruno didn't need to say it.

With a final sympathetic look, Bruno left, and Rye first sagged against the wall, then forced himself upright and to walk away. The picture Bruno had painted, Rye had caught hints of it in the looks in the eyes of his fellow Rangers, or in the way their glances had slid from him, their gazes not holding his. And the outline that LeGrande had been sketching — join the dots and that was the picture it made.

But that wasn't what had gone down. Not exactly. Chip had been checking out the place, just like Rye had, only then he walked up to the shed and... Rye's thoughts slowed. What Bruno had said and LeGrande had intimated — things could be twisted to look like that. "Could be re-formed," he whispered. He slowed his steps. Where the fuck was he? Near the chapel, which seemed as good a place as any to go right now, with his head in a fog. Chip's body was laid there...

...and Chip's wife was there. *Nope, not wife. Widow.* All in black and sitting near the plain wooden coffin. Lina. As if she'd heard him call her name, she looked up. Her hands were clutching a large rosary, its bead chain tangled around her fingers. She didn't speak, just let a tear run down her face.

"Lina." Rye swept his hat off and looked around, spotting a box of paper tissues on the small table at the top of the alcove. He grabbed a handful and brought them for her. "Get y'all some water?"

Her face twisted and she shook her head. *Yeah, what good will a plastic cup of water do?*

"I'm so sorry," Rye whispered. They'd spoken on the phone last night. He'd wanted to tell her, although she'd already been informed officially of course. "And sorry I couldn't come over last night. By the time I got through, it was this morning."

She nodded and patted the chair next to her. Rye sat. They'd always had an easy relationship, joking, teasing and mock-flirting. "You tell yourself as a serving lawman's wife that you accept the risk, the danger, you know?" Lina sniffed. "But maybe it's more that you *fool* yourself. Whatever, you don't expect it."

"I know." What more could Rye say? They sat in silence for a while, Lina giving the occasional dab to her eyes. Rye shifted in his seat and his foot knocked against something. Lina's purse, he discovered, bending to see what he'd disturbed. He handed it to her. "Sorry. Looks new and now my boot print's on it."

"It's fine." Lina nevertheless wiped it with a Kleenex. "Yeah, it's new."

"Classy-looking," Rye offered. What did he know about fashion? "Designer?" Well, yeah, there was one word he knew.

"It is." Lina's half-smile looked twisted. "From that little outlet mall in San Antonio. Chip got me a whole lot of new things lately, little presents to make up for being away so much, out of town on that case."

She was still brushing her purse and not looking at Rye, who was glad about that, because his face probably looked as stunned as he felt. "What—?" he started.

"Oh, I know you can't talk about it." Lina sighed. "But I think he felt guilty at having to be away so often, you know?"

"And he got you gifts." Rye felt like he was doing a jigsaw puzzle with no illustration to guide him. In the dark. With gloves on.

"I joked that he must be getting good travel expenses and he confessed that it was winnings. He had a winning streak. We've had money lately for a change." A hardness crossed Lina's face. "Well, I knew when I married him that he liked to gamble."

"A flutter. He liked a flutter." Chip's father had been Irish, and that was what he'd called betting or games of chance. Rye always remembered the crazy name.

"Did you go with him?"

"To…"

"The Lucky Card Club. Oh, forget I asked. It doesn't matter, does it. Nothing matters now. Not the bigger house we were planning on buying now the mortgage is paid off, or the boat Chip was dreaming about." Lina turned back to the coffin. "And I know y'all can't make promises, but if you can, this assignment, case, whatever it is—I'd like y'all to finish it. For him."

Rye gave a nod, but the motion was a lie. He couldn't finish the assignment, the case, the mission— whatever it should be called…because there wasn't one. They hadn't been working any such thing in San Antonio or anywhere else outside of Waco. Why had Chip told his wife they were? For a brief second, Rye wondered if Chip had been assigned some hush-hush duty with a different partner. No. That wasn't how they worked.

The obvious answer was that if a married guy was spending time elsewhere, he had his own reasons for it. *Commonly called a sidepiece.* Rye didn't buy that, not about Chip. And it didn't explain the money. Or Chip's behavior yesterday. Suspicion slithered in Rye, cold and slow and making him sick to his stomach.

He was almost glad his cell buzzed a summons, a reminder of the meeting scheduled with the company's senior captain, Chief Fischer, and the headquarters captain, Assistant Chief Pereira, although he wasn't looking forward to it any. He'd been right not to. The two men took him through it all again, with even more pauses and looks at each other than LeGrande and his team had made.

"I did not leave my partner without backup so that he was ambushed, sir!" Rye shouted. "He—" About to say *walked right on up to the targets*, he stopped himself. He'd be accusing a Texas Ranger who'd died in the line of duty of working for a cartel, for Christ's sake! It could not be true.

But...but if it was, would Chip be the only one? Law enforcement here in Waco could get nothing on Amaral or any of the Camargo cartel, and cocaine and amphetamines continued to flood into the city. "That is not what happened. Whatever it looks like."

"Well, it *looks* unfortunate. The media's gonna be all over this." Pereira took another glance at Fischer. "We have discussed suspension, for failing in your duty."

"The hell? Excuse me, sirs, but that's bullshit!" Rye exploded.

"Another alternative is leave. For counseling—"

"I don't want that." Rye's answer was quick. He didn't want any kind of therapy. He'd refused it when his parents were killed in a car accident when he was a teen, figuring the time was better spent getting on with the task of caring for his younger sister at the same time as he finished school and worked at jobs to support them.

"Y'all want me out of the picture till it blows over? Signed off of active duty?" Rye was getting paranoid, thinking every single person in this building could be in on this. "Out of town?"

He gazed over their heads at the state map on the wall behind them. He'd seen it more times than he could remember, but now his gaze was drawn to San Antonio and an airfield marked on it. Springs Airfield. Springs...*fuentes*, in Spanish. What if the name he'd heard the cartel members ask about wasn't a person, but a place, and the place the drugs had been flying in from?

"San Antonio."

The name Fischer said seemed to have been plucked from inside Rye's head, and he fought not to react apart from a "Sir?"

"We said we'd send someone..." Fischer spoke before Pereira could. "How do you feel about guard duty, Ryland? Or more correctly, escort duty? A temporary assignment out of town, in San Antonio?"

"I'll take it." He didn't care what bullshit assignment this was, or who or what he was guarding or escorting, and nodded along at the description of the temporary loan of historical items from the Texas Ranger Hall of Fame and Museum here in Waco to something called the Buckhorn. He'd take any excuse to look into what Chip had been doing.

In San Antonio...

Chapter Five

"Are you feeling Lucky?"

Jonas wondered how many people made that tired old joke when they came to this card club. He hadn't. If anyone made it to him, he'd follow it with "Depends...he got a nice ass?"

"Joe." Jonas—Joe here—got a nod from whoever was on duty on the Lucky Card Club door. He couldn't remember this guy. Did the man recall him or was he just going by Jonas' membership card? No, the man was another new face, one of many that the place turned over. Jonas had a good memory. It was essential for card games, even in places like this dump, which wasn't anything like as flashy as the Palace, the casino Jonas had been in with Elliot.

He wanted to grin, remembering Elliot's amazement at seeing another facet to the earnest, knowledgeable antiques-loving Jonas. Jonas had pretended to be some more-money-than-brains wealthy guy from Dallas, half-drunk and out for a good time, thinking he was a high-roller. He'd even brought along a cuddly toy as his lucky charm, which the management had removed from him and checked for hidden cameras. *Well, to be fair, a teddy-cam is a thing.* A thing that Jonas didn't have, however—he relied on counting cards to win.

That was for blackjack, of course. He had other techniques for poker.

If Elliot were here with him now, he'd see yet another side to Jonas, someone a lot more down to earth not to mention earthy, dressed in black jeans and not the smart pants he wore at the store or college, wearing contact lenses rather than his black-framed glasses…and going by the name of Joe.

He came here from time to time, to gamble and hook up. He ordered a beer—it was safer to get bottled here, and drink from the bottle—and nodded at a couple of guys he knew, Ze included. He was one of the better casual fucks Jonas, as Joe, had enjoyed. He was a possibility, once Jonas had worked off some other feelings, dealt with different needs. He looked toward the gaming tables.

"Going for the Big O?" Ze asked, sliding another beer to Jonas.

Jonas took it, tipped it toward Ze in thanks and nodded. He felt like playing Omaha and made for the table. Ze took a seat too, but Jonas knew he'd fold soon. Jonas finished his first beer and chugged half the second, settling in, but he'd only played a couple of hands when the atmosphere changed.

He didn't know exactly how, beyond feeling that the air had thinned somehow, but when he looked up, it was into the bluest pair of eyes he'd ever seen. He could see the sky in them. No, not exactly that. More like they were used to looking at the whole horizon. *What does that even mean?*

Jonas wasn't given to flights of fancy. He was more analytical, so tried to understand. Maybe it was the lines fanning out from the corners of the eyes, like their owner regularly squinted? And what about their owner, the possessor of those big-sky eyes? Jonas stifled a gasp. Hands down, the blond was the sexiest thing Jonas had ever seen.

He's a cowboy. What else could Jonas think of the tall, broad, tan guy in tight jeans and roper boots, with a high-crowned, wide-brimmed hat under his arm? A native of Dallas, Jonas knew better than to use terms such as *western boots* or *Stetson* inaccurately. He'd been watching too long — the man, who'd been gazing about the place, must have felt Jonas' stare, because his head turned slowly, slowly, then slower still, until he locked eyes with Jonas, his searching blue gaze pinning Jonas in his seat.

Unrelenting, was the next thought to cross Jonas' mind. The guy lifted his beer bottle to his lips, and Jonas' rapt stare took in the way his throat worked as he swallowed. Drinking left his lips shiny and made his tongue tip peep out to lick up a stray drop. He had to be doing that on purpose, to make Jonas tighten in his jeans, his cock doing its best to salute the stranger.

"Hey…" The dealer's voice recalled Jonas to what he was sitting at the table to do, but he hadn't been following the game, much less counting the outs, so he folded. He kept his eyes on the table but knew the guy was coming over. Jonas could swear he heard the clip of the man's bootheels, even though the place was carpeted, as he sauntered across. As the man approached, Jonas inhaled.

Leather sweetened with gunpowder and overlaid with tobacco and sagebrush. Jonas opened eyes he didn't know he'd closed and found the cowboy quirking a dark-blond eyebrow at him.

"You in?"

The dealer's question made Jonas start and he nodded. *Damn.* The first rule of any card game was pay attention to the game. Another rule was to sit so he was last to act on the hand, which gave him knowledge about what kind of hands his opponents had. Adding that to an ability to remember all the cards he'd seen that affected his and the other players outs usually meant he played his cards well, winning without bluffing.

The swing of a chair near him was the stranger swiveling it to sit on it the wrong way round. This normally irritated Jonas, but it looked natural to the blond. Jonas risked a peep to see if the man was leaning on the back rest. He was, looking like he was sitting in a saddle, resting on its horn. Well, fine. The guy wasn't playing, but Jonas would show him he had his own area of expertise. He knew a couple of players so was aware of their tells, how they played in each pot.

The guy to his left overvalued suited cards. Contrary to popular belief, flushes weren't that common, and the poor guy limped in with a small-suited two pair, which Jonas beat with a straight, his warm-up to a full house in the next hand.

"You're good."

The stranger's voice was deep and had a drawl. Normally, in a place like this, it would have been a come-on, an opener to which Jonas could respond with a murmured "You've no idea *how* good," or "Yeah, I'm *real* good with my hands," or something equally slutty, but there was nothing sleazy about the guy's manner or gaze when it met his.

So Jonas muttered a "Thanks" and focused on winning his hand, which he did with a four of a kind. His two opponents around the table were predictable, so he was able to up that to a ten-high straight flush in the next hand.

"The fuck?" The guy to his left was on his feet as Jonas scooped the pot toward him. "That's not right."

"It is. A straight beats—" the dealer began.

"I know that, *idiot*." The loser cut the dealer off. "I mean this motherfucker's cheating! He has to be."

"Or I'm a better player?" Jonas replied, the adrenaline rush of the situation even better than that of winning at poker.

The guy slammed both hands down on the table, sending cards and chips flying, then lunged for Jonas' winnings, screaming abuse and accusations. *Shit.* Was he armed? Jonas didn't carry, so didn't know if the place obliged patrons to check their weapons in a locker before they went in. But he'd bet the dealers and bar staff were carrying and that the situation would escalate.

"Hey."

With that one laconic syllable, delivered as he flowed to his feet, the cowboy had the attention of everyone around the table, Jonas' opponent included. Jonas blinked, because the next he knew, the blond guy was behind the sore loser, imprisoning his arms behind his back and kicking his legs into a spread. The jerk's face hit the table sideways and a knife spun from his hand, clattering among the poker chips.

Jonas barely got out of the way before the man who'd been on the door raced up, along with another employee presumably charged with security. The blond dragged his prisoner over to one side, beckoning the guards with a *come here* motion.

"He's all yours," he said, handing the guy over. "Fucker was armed."

Exclamations rang out then, people unfreezing.

"See that, Joe?" Ze cried.

Jonas nodded, brushing Ze off, annoyed that the interruption meant he'd lost some of what the stranger and Lucky Cards staff were saying. He strained to hear. Something about the blond being in law enforcement, from out of town?

"Friend o'mine, name of Chip Daniels, came here too. Think he was well-known around these parts?" the cowboy drawled, looking from one man to the other.

"You…better come see the boss," the guy from the door said, after a pause, indicating a door to one side and nodding to his co-worker to deal with the jerk.

"I'd like that," the blond replied. Before he strutted off, he turned to look back at Jonas.

Jonas expected a *"you okay?"* or *"it's all over now,"* but the stranger just looked, and the heat in his gaze burned Jonas to the core. That blue gaze held promise, and Jonas was going to make sure it was delivered on. He raised an eyebrow and got a crooked half-grin in exchange before the guy swung away. *Right.*

"No, I'm fine," Jonas assured the dealer and everyone else who crowded around him. He pushed a heap of his chips back across the table. "Why don't we all get a drink?" He stayed long enough to knock back a whiskey and was in the small entranceway, waiting, when the cowboy sauntered through, stopping at the sight of Jonas.

"So, cowboy," Jonas began.

"Rye," the guy corrected. "Joe, right?"

"Rye..." Jonas let it roll around his tongue, much like the drink, ignoring the question. "I haven't thanked you."

"That right?" Rye's eyes were half-hooded now, the look in them speculative. "So y'all gonna?"

Assuming he'd read every signal correct, Jonas gave a nod and walked down the short corridor, in the opposite direction to the entrance. "This way."

He gestured for Rye to exit first, and when Rye went to move past him, Jonas pressed close, inhaling that outdoorsy scent and the recent fumes of whiskey as cheap as that he'd just drunk—the boss must have given Rye a free drink. Him pushing against Rye made him stumble, Jonas following as if glued to him, so they arrived in the back alley face to face...and cock to cock.

Jonas was glad he couldn't see his own face because he knew the expression on it would be predatory. Rye was hard, tenting his tight jeans, and Jonas reached for him slowly enough for Rye to stop him. Rye didn't. He slammed the palms of his hands flat against the wall behind him and thrust out his crotch to meet Jonas' hand. He was big. Jonas licked his lips and dropped to his knees. He had Rye's jeans undone and shoved down along with his boxers in seconds. Rye hissed, maybe at the cool evening air, and Jonas grabbed the base of his thick, meaty cock and sucked the crown into his mouth. He had it releasing pre-cum in an instant.

Rye gasped but didn't pull away as Jonas coated his taste buds in Rye's bitter salt. He tongued the slit and cupped Rye's balls, rolling the sac in his palm as a warning a heartbeat before he sucked Rye's cock to the back of his throat. He hummed, making Rye groan and his hands leave the wall to fist in Jonas' hair. Jonas looked up, trying to catch Rye's eyes in the half light, wanting to tell him not to hold back.

Rye got the signal. He thrust, holding Jonas' head still, fucking his hard dick into Jonas' willing mouth and ready throat. Ignoring the punishing ground under his knees, Jonas reveled in each push and bump, and when Rye started pumping harder, faster, he laved the little bundle of nerves on the underside of the crown, wanting to make Rye cry out.

Rye did, and was grunting with each thrust now, punishing Jonas' throat and lips. He'd feel it later but didn't care, not when things were this hot. He squeezed Rye's balls and Rye's thrusts became short, jerky stabs. His fingers clenching in Jonas' hair pulled the strands painfully, his version of a last-second warning before he shouted and buried his cock deep. Jonas felt the first warm spurt of cum in his throat and managed to pull his head so Rye's load filled his mouth. It nearly made him come in his pants too—he'd never climaxed without some stimulation to his dick when blowing a guy, but this was a close thing. He swallowed, drinking Rye down.

His release left Rye, the big tough cowboy, trembling. Jonas let him go, staring him in the eye. Rye jerked, visibly pulling himself together. He yanked his pants and boxers up as Jonas got to his feet, the silence stretching.

"Well, hell if I ain't clairvoyant." Rye ran a hand through his hair. "Said you were good, didn't I?" The plains-wide smile that took over his face was so beautiful it made Jonas blink.

"You have no idea," he murmured in reply. This was the part of the night when he'd want his own itch scratched, or to leave. He paused then hesitated, not wanting to break this connection. He didn't understand it, but it was there.

"Joe…" Rye started.

No. There couldn't be any false pretenses. "Jonas." Jonas pointed his thumb at his chest. *Me.*

"Jonas." Rye's grin said he liked the name. "That was fuckin' amazing but I don't want this to carry on or end here. Come back to my motel with me?"

Chapter Six

The car pulled off the road and onto a gravel surface. Rye got the feeling he'd taken the guy—Jonas, he'd said?—by surprise. Hell, he'd surprised himself. But what he'd said was true. He didn't want whatever was between them to continue here and for damn sure not end here either.

Jonas recovered quickly though. "Oh. You think I'm a pushover because I got on my knees to you?"

"I...no. I don't think you're a pushover." He fucking hoped the guy wasn't. Rye was a lawman, strong and unflinching in the face of all the shit he dealt with...and he craved to not be the one making the decisions. Jonas calling the shots just now, making Rye take what he meted out, had meant Rye could let go, in a way he rarely did and sorely needed.

He stared at Jonas, hoping the man could read his eyes even in this poor light and see the desires there. "I think...you're in control."

Jonas tilted his head back. "Damn right I am." He led the way out of the alley and Rye, heart skipping in relief, followed. "Where's your motel?"

"Couple streets away." Rye looked around, orientating himself.

"You're not from here." Jonas scanned him from head to toe, from Greeley hat to Lucchese boots. "Austin? Houston? Garland?"

Rye hadn't mentioned in Jonas' hearing that he was a Ranger, only that he was a lawman, but was it that obvious, that Jonas was listing the cities of the different Companies' HQs?

"Waco?" Jonas continued. "Oh, Waco it is."

Rye started a little. *Good thing I didn't go up against the guy in a hand of poker, the way he can read tells a guy don't know he has.* "Yeah. Gabe Ryland, Field Ranger, Company F, Waco. Howdy." It was weird to be offering his hand to the guy who'd just given him the best head he'd ever gotten—so good Rye was proud he could control the trembling in his legs and walk normally—and for that guy to shake it, but it was that kind of night. "Folks call me Rye. They call you Joe?"

"No. I'm Jonas."

The command in his voice had Rye nodding in obedience.

"So, what's a nice guy like you doing in a neighborhood like this?" Jonas deadpanned as they walked.

Rye saw what he meant. These streets didn't appear in guides to the city's attractions. "Sure I'm a nice guy?" he queried.

"Hmm. I'd say so? Well, a good guy." Jonas jerked his chin at Rye's hat, light enough to be classed as white, the classic marker of a hero. "But I'm hoping you're nasty too."

"So, iffen I answer your question with 'looking to get fucked'…" Rye let the reply dangle. They'd reached his truck.

"I'd say I'll follow you there, but once there, I take the lead." Jonas appraised him by the seedy glow of a streetlamp, and, *thank fuck*, seemed to like what he saw. "Usual code system, green for go, yellow for slow or pause, red for stop?"

Rye dropped his gaze, and nodded, not caring it looked too damn eager. He got into his vehicle, waited for Jonas to pull up alongside in a Jetta, and headed on out, anticipation beating like a drum inside him. Was this stupid? It was certainly risky. He didn't know the first thing about the guy, except that he wanted him. Because the things Jonas wanted to do to Rye, Rye wanted too. He'd never felt such a connection before, and hadn't thought it was possible, with a stranger.

It didn't take him long to be pulling into the courtyard — or so the info on the place called it — of his motel, and he parked as close to his room as possible. "It ain't exactly the Hilton," he mumbled when Jonas joined him.

"It ain't exactly a No-Tell Motel either," Jonas replied.

True. The place didn't rent rooms by the hour. "You mockin' me?" Rye asked with a grin.

"Are you mocking yourself?" Jonas flashed back.

His words had Rye pausing as he shoved his shoulder into the door to help it open. Maybe he was, a little. Hiding behind an exaggerated version of himself.

"Well don't."

The sharpness in Jonas' voice pulled Rye up.

"I expect frankness," he continued.

"And...obedience?" Rye asked, his voice only a shade above a whisper.

"Turn around."

Rye's body obeyed the command before his brain processed it, and he was once again body to body with Jonas. "Exactly," Jonas purred, right in Rye's ear and let that hang, thick with promise, before he trailed his mouth from Rye's lobe down his neck to where it met his shoulder...and bit. Hard, or at least hard enough to make his point. At the same time, he reached around to grab a handful of Rye's ass and pressed his groin into Rye's.

The sensory overload left Rye dazed, and a smile tickled at Jonas' lips. "You'll do fine," he said, thrusting his hips to get Rye inside.

Once in the room, Rye stepped away from Jonas, using the space to gather himself together. He locked the creaking door then switched on the lamps in the low-ceilinged room, revealing its outdated, mismatched fixtures and décor. He'd stayed in worse. This one was clean, no bloodstains on the coverlet, no bullet holes in the walls and no rodent droppings or poison or carcasses below the sink or in the closet. The mattress was thin, but he'd seen no bedbugs or roaches when he'd examined it earlier.

Would Jonas ask what he was doing in town? Someone coming for a city break would stay somewhere nicer, wouldn't they? But apart from a cursory glance around, Jonas wasn't sparing any attention for the room. He was checking out Rye and fuck if Rye wasn't getting a boner again, under that appraisal and slow lick of the lips. The bitemark throbbed, and he got a hand to it, half-expecting to feel blood or see it on his fingertips, but Jonas hadn't broken the skin. Skilled, he'd just left his mark that Rye would be wearing, hidden by his collar, but there.

"Strip," Jonas ordered. "And God, it's such a cliché, but yeah, you can leave your hat on."

There was no music, sleazy or otherwise, but its lack didn't make this feel clinical or routine. Not the way Jonas' heated brown gaze held Rye's, Jonas only looking his body over once Rye stood naked. Then Jonas stepped nearer.

"Rye, you have the sexiest nipples."

Did he? He'd never thought about it. He was about to ask why or how but Jonas pinched the tips, and the flare of pain shot straight to Rye's balls, turning whatever question he might have had into a strangled yelp. Still holding Rye's gaze, Jonas pinched again, and this time he twisted, *he fucking twisted*, which dialed up the burn…that Rye wanted more of.

"Fuck," he gasped, locking his knees so he didn't collapse when the pain turned into nerve-tingling pleasure.

"When I say so," Jonas reprimanded, and pulled on Rye's nipples, keeping up the pressure. "Love these. I could play all night."

Rye didn't think it was possible, but Jonas managed to twist *tighter*, making Rye hiss out his discomfort…and lean forward to give Jonas better access to bring more.

"And here's me without my clamps." Jonas tsked at the fact. "Pity. Oh. You like that idea."

He did and it was easy to understand what tell of his had given *this* away—perhaps the stiffening of his dick, for all Jonas had made him come and come fucking hard not twenty minutes ago.

"You like getting fucked when you're in clamps?" Jonas asked, his voice almost conversational, which made the things he was saying even hotter. "Like having them unscrewed just when you come, so the release is off the scale?" He twisted harder. "So you get the pain with the pleasure?"

Rye, supposedly a big strong Texas Ranger, whimpered. He fucking *whimpered*, but it seemed it was the right answer.

"Look at you just about ready to fall apart for me. Oh, but I'm not fucking you until you come again," Jonas told him. "Yes, I should have said…"

He hadn't forgotten. It was part of the game. Rye had played this game before, but not at this level. Not with such a master directing play, dictating the moves.

"And you're wearing my mark." Jonas leaned it and licked at the bruise he'd made, then blew on the wetness. "Did it hurt when I made it?"

Rye shuddered, having trouble concentrating when Jonas continued working his nipples. "Uh," he got out, his thready tone and full, flushed cock conveying *fuck yes*.

"So you liked it."

Rye should have heard a warning in that, but Jonas bending to take one distended nub between his teeth and clamping down took all his attention. Clenching his teeth so he didn't bellow out loud, he grabbed for Jonas' head, confused if he wanted him to stop or carry on.

Jonas went with Option B, increasing the pain while he did so, mainly by squeezing Rye's free nipple, the one he wasn't biting, to apply equal pressure to that too. *Shit.*

"I'm gonna..." Rye gasped out. But he couldn't come again so soon, could he? And without any stimulation to his dick?

And fuck if Jonas didn't half-turn, to rub his hip against Rye's dick, bringing sudden, hard friction to Rye's throbbing cock. "Go," he ordered, and Rye just about wrapped his hand around himself before he blew — with Jonas squeezing and biting his nipples all through it, making Rye's climax the longest and sharpest he'd ever had.

The second it finally ended, Rye panting and wrung out, was when Jonas pushed him backward, onto the bed. As he landed and bounced, losing his hat somewhere along the way, Jonas stripped. Rye wished his vision was working properly so he could appreciate Jonas' solid body, but he'd come so hard that things were still a little whited-out around the edges.

Jonas dug around in his pocket for condoms and lube.

"Turn over," he ordered, and Rye scrambled to obey. "Let me see that ass. Yeah, best ass in the club this evening. Show it off for me." He kneeled on the bed between Rye's legs and jerked him into the position he wanted — ass up, shoulders down, knees spread wider.

Rye was vulnerable, spent, covered in his own sticky cum and at the mercy of a man he'd just met, but his heart was singing a song of utter joy.

"You must be sensitive here." Jonas held his balls. Just cradled them, maybe waiting for Rye to say *yellow* or even *red*. But Rye didn't. "I see."

Maybe Jonas did, understood that in his job, his life, Rye had to maintain such control that he craved to hand it over during sex. He tightened his hand, and Rye cried out at the dull ache spreading up from his balls to his ass and even his cock, which — fuck, *what?* — was trying to stir again.

Feeling warm breath on his skin, Rye tensed, holding himself rigid in something like disbelief...a second before Jonas pulled one ass cheek aside and glided a warm, knowing tongue down his crack. Rye pressed his face into the pillow to muffle a moan.

Jonas chuckled. "Yeah, going to make you scream for me," he promised right before scraping his teeth over Rye's hole. When Jonas' tongue penetrated him, tasting him, Rye gripped the bedclothes beneath him savagely enough to rip them. Then Jonas stopped.

Because Rye was still floating, his eyes squeezed closed and his mouth open at the sheer bliss of being rimmed, it took the loss a few seconds to register. He was too far gone to interpret any noise — meaning he was unprepared when a second later, Jonas shoved lubed fingers into his ass.

Rye didn't scream, but only just and because he fought against it, as best he could through the jagged bliss of Jonas fingering him, subjecting him to rough, hard thrusts, bumping his knuckles against Rye's outer rim with each in and out, and his fingertips over Rye's gland with each push. Rye's shivers became shudders, especially as Jonas kept his rhythm erratic and unpredictable, leaving Rye clueless about *what* and *when* and *how hard* and *how deep*. He started to shake. Jonas slid his hand free.

"Turn over."

Rye tried to obey the barked order, and Jonas helped him thud onto his back. He arranged him higher up the bed, and with no warning, lined up his cock with Rye's waiting ass and thrust. Rye came nearer to a scream than he'd gotten all night at the sudden hard penetration.

"Okay?" Jonas panted, and at Rye's tight nod, bent Rye's legs into his chest and pounded deep into his ass.

Jesus, he was big, almost too big, just like Rye was almost too full. And the sensation, when Jonas bent to pinch a nipple again? That had Rye climaxing but not coming, seeing as he had no cum left. His dick hadn't got the memo though. Rye felt battered by the onslaught, Jonas slamming his hole, abusing his tender nub…then bending down to bite his lower neck again, in the same place.

Rye's cock spluttered out a drop of cum, all he had to give, his tribute to the waves of climax dragging at him. Jonas' release was longer, hot and strong pulses in Rye's ass that he felt even through the condom. Rye forced his eyes open and stared straight into Jonas', staring back at him.

Eventually, Jonas moved, withdrawing carefully, holding on to the base of the condom, and Rye had to fight not to curl his legs around him, to hold Jonas, as sweat-soaked and wild-haired as he knew he must be, to him. "You…" His mouth was too dry to speak.

"You okay?" Jonas had to swallow and cough to speak too.

"You didn't make me scream. So…" *We should do this again*, Rye wanted to say. Because he wanted to. Wanted to see this man again. And again. And the way Jonas was looking at him, that expression in his eyes, did it mean he felt the same? "I ain't never felt anything like that," he said. Jonas had wanted frankness, right?

"It…was something else," Jonas agreed, moving to the edge of the mattress, and not into Rye's arms.

"Can I see you again?" burst from Rye. "There's something—we got something. And it—"

"I don't…" Jonas waved a hand from Rye to himself. "I'm not looking…" He appeared torn. "How long are you in town for?"

"A while." Rye sat, every cell in his body leaping toward Jonas.

"Me too." Jonas gave an attempt at a smile. "So let's leave it to fate? If we meet again, then we'll see where this takes us?"

Well, shit. It was like the sun had gone in, and all Rye could do was grab on to this one tiny illusory gleam.

He nodded because what else could he do?

Chapter Seven

The upper parts of every wall in the salon were studded with mounted animal heads. Jonas looked from one to another, trying to understand the principle behind the display. *Subspecies? Size? Color?* Too bleary-eyed to discern, he walked farther inside the building and into a smaller section, where a longhorn steer with *really* long horns squinted at Jonas from its corral. He eyed it back, glad it was stuffed.

The next alcove held art made from rattlesnake rattles. He hadn't even known there was such a thing, but there was, 3D too, the rattles stuck onto card like kids did with macaroni. Even the sign announcing this particular display was made from them. *Am I in the right place?* He'd never been here before. Another board pointed him toward something the place called a *Carnival of Curiosities*, and he shook his head.

Was this why Lucia had called him earlier and asked him to go in her place? He hadn't really been able to refuse. She not only ranked higher than him in the department, being an assistant professor and so on the tenure track, but was a sort of friend too.

Jonas wasn't really that sure what her title of Special Collections Coordinator meant, but when she'd called first thing, one of her children — or all of them, for all he knew — screaming and crying in the background, he'd groggily agreed to help. He'd said he'd go along and be the someone from the department assuring anyone concerned of the historical importance of the items that a small local museum was receiving on loan. And yes, he'd assist in displaying them if necessary.

"It's more your area anyway, American history," Lucia had shouted, over the wailing and sobbing. *"Frontiers?"*

As a dog was barking along with the child yelling, he'd thought she'd said "front ears" then missed her next few words while he puzzled that out.

"So could even be something you want to write about," Lucia had wheedled.

"Write a — ? Oh." Jonas had got it. She meant publish. The key to getting on, as was aptly said, was to publish or perish, to come up with some novel but more importantly high-impact research because an article in an academic journal was a quantifiable metric to be evaluated by, for promotion.

"And it might give you more ideas for that course you were planning, about engaging with history through objects and artworks?"

Lucia had liked Jonas' idea and had listened to him expound on it, her reactions giving him valuable feedback. For that if nothing else he would have helped her out, but of course couldn't refuse a beleaguered mother of what seemed like a dozen kids screeching and moaning.

"Oh, hello?" Jonas spotted a man in a suit and ran after him. "Are you the curator?"

"The what now? I'm the guide," the guy said, his handlebar mustache quivering.

God, Jonas hated realizing how much of a snob he'd become. "Good morning, sir. I'm from the Hill. Laurel Heights, I mean. The university?" He'd stupidly given the college's nickname. Well, he was off to a good start.

"Oh, the history lady! Well, gent, I guess...." The old man eyed him, not letting his disappointment show. "To see what we're getting?" He smiled, warm and genuine. "Want a coffee and the tour?"

Jonas wanted the former — *needed* the former — and guessed he had no choice about the latter. Grateful for the caffeine, he nodded at the story he was told, about the history of the place, the Wild West salon that had started from cowboys getting a shot of whiskey or a beer in exchange for the horns and antlers that the eccentric owner liked to collect.

It was interesting, and the place could possibly be a good one for Heights' students to carry out field work, should his summer course become a reality, or even for them to do placements at, if by some miracle his course ideas were accepted. Jonas sighed, selfishly wishing he had time and leisure to wallow in his memories of last night. He didn't usually. He was into one-and-done hookups, and with the blue-collar guys he met in the kind of bars and clubs unlikely to feature in San Antonio's top ten lists.

But that guy last night... *Gabe. Rye.* Jonas could see his narrowed blue eyes, set in a tan face and topped with that dark-blond hair, as if the man himself was right in front of him. That he'd been tall and broad-shouldered, muscled but not bulky and had had the sweetest ass Jonas had seen in a good while hadn't hurt any, either.

But beyond the physical, there'd been that electric zing, the pull of a connection, and not just because the guy had rescued Jonas from that jerk of an opponent who'd objected to losing to him. Although that had been something in itself. Jonas shivered at the memory. He really had to stop that stupid thrill-seeking, that pathetic chasing of an adrenaline rush.

But there had been something between them. And what had Jonas done? Well, he'd given his real name, which he didn't usually do, but had muttered something stupid about leaving things in the lap of the gods, hadn't he? *Jeez.* Could he be any more lame? *Is there a god of hookups?*

Jonas wanted to smack himself upside the head for his behavior. How big was San Antonio? How many people either lived in the city or came into it every day to work? The numbers, the statistics, were against him. He wasn't likely to see that Texas Ranger…

…Museum? *"Texas Ranger Museum?"* Jonas, taken to another room, repeated his guide's words as he looked around what he took to be a to-scale diorama, or recreated stage set, his eyes bugging.

"Well, sure!" His guide indicated the delights awaiting Jonas over the threshold. "Welcome to Ranger Town, pardner! We got a jail cell, blacksmith shop and a replica of the Bonnie and Clyde getaway car." He led Jonas in. "And authentic Texas Ranger Division artifacts, like handguns, shotguns, badges, photographs… You won't see a finer recreation of San Antonio at the turn of the century—you came through the saloon, right?"

Saloon. Not salon, Jonas belatedly realized. His heart rate picked up, his senses prickling. "And this is where those new items, the new exhibits…" He could hardly get his words out and they failed him altogether when voices called, footsteps rang out and a uniformed security team entered, carrying chests and strongboxes…and led by —

Gabe 'Rye' Ryland. Who took off his western hat, revealing slicked-back blond hair that Jonas knew how it looked messy, just as he knew how that tan skin looked dewed in sweat, those blue eyes closed in ecstasy and that crooked smile twisted into a pleasure-pain grimace. Pleasure and pain that Jonas had brought him. Gabe's swaggering footsteps came to a halt.

"*Jonas?*" he asked, at the same time as Jonas said "*Rye?*" The disbelief in Rye's tone matched that in Jonas' and was reflected in Rye's blue-eyed gaze and mirrored what must be written all over Jonas' face. A slow frown of suspicion crossed his handsome face.

"I'm a professor," burst from Jonas. "I'm here from the college, because of…" He made a vague gesture around him in proof that it was a coincidence, that he wasn't stalking this man.

"And I'm a Texas Ranger." Rye patted the official circle star badge pinned above his left shirt pocket then took a couple steps forward. "Here because of…" He pointed at the chests and his lopsided smile took over his face, banishing the steely-eyed frown.

"But I —" Jonas didn't get the chance to complete whatever he'd been going to say — and he wasn't sure what that was — before they were interrupted.

In the hours that followed, Jonas couldn't stop staring, his gaze returning to Rye again and again, as Rye's did him, and he hated that the demands of what they were both there to do broke it. The bustle of the museum guides arranging the loan items irritated Jonas, as did the calls on his supposed expertise about the yellowing sepia photographs and old diaries and official accounts. Every time he went to speak to Rye, something happened to prevent it, but that pull, that electricity, zapped through Jonas, and he felt, through Rye too.

A lull came, and, determined, Jonas took a step toward Rye. They'd spoken about leaving things up to fate—well, what was this if not that very thing?

"Professor...Abrams, right?"

Jonas looked around at the girl's voice. They'd had reporters from a couple of local TV and radio programs—the museum was good at PR—which was how Jonas had learned that Rye was on temporary secondment from the official Ranger Museum with this loan exhibition, but this girl looked too young to work for any media outlet.

"We met at Mighty Heights Radio Station," she continued, then looked around the museum. "Does the college have a link with this institution?"

"Well, I'm, erm..." Jonas saw Rye paying attention. Their eyes met and Jonas could not, *would not* let whatever it was they had drop. He wanted to be near this man. "I'll be attached to the exhibition, yes. I'm researching an article for an academic publication" — he'd have to thank Lucia for that idea. Maybe babysit or dog-sit for her—"and I'm piloting ideas here for a course I'm developing that I'll be teaching about taking a closer look at American history through the study of objects in a collection."

"That sounds interesting. How would it work?"

The question came in a drawl, and Rye, standing wide-legged with his thumbs tucked into his belt that had Jonas shifting to conceal his erection, seemed interested.

"Well, it'll be experiential, allowing students to scrutinize objects and artworks through a critical lens," Jonas replied to him. "Everything has a story." *And everyone*, he thought. "Oh, and students will also be able to gain understanding of a functioning museum, engaging with curators and staff and the public." He included the guides in his words as he said them.

"Sounds real good." Rye nodded.

It did. Well, that was his dream, anyway. Then it was his turn to watch Rye at work, when the first lot of visitors, a school party, came in, all of whom were thrilled to meet a genuine Texas Ranger, one there to answer their questions, seemingly. Jonas had things to do, but couldn't tear himself away, learning that most Rangers, Rye included, came from the Texas Highway Patrol, which was also part of the Department of Public Safety and that yeah, Rangers could be considered to be like the FBI in their scope.

Time passed and things were winding down and he couldn't think of excuses to stay any longer. The items were displayed invitingly, their positioning allowing for maximum interaction, and melding with the existing exhibition. Jonas clicked his briefcase shut and was about to stand from the small desk he'd been working at when a shadow fell across him. Without looking up, he knew who it was.

"'The will or principle or determining cause by which things in general are believed to come to be as they are or events to happen as they do'," Rye said.

"Excuse me?" Jonas blinked.

"'An inevitable outcome, condition or end'," Rye replied.

"Are you...quoting a definition of the word *fate*?" Jonas couldn't believe it.

"Thought I'd best look it up, y'all being an educated college teacher and me just a simple—"

"You're not 'just' anything," Jonas interrupted. Yes, he was educated, and yes, he did seek out uncomplicated one-nighters with men who weren't, but that didn't make him any better than this man standing before him, his hat in his hands.

"Well, anyways, knowledge ain't never wasted." Rye shrugged. "You said, leave it to fate and…" He indicated himself and Jonas. "Now, I ain't much of a poker player…"

He'd lost Jonas again, while charming him all over again. "Go on?"

"But I'd like to put my cards on the table," Rye continued. "I never felt anything like I felt last night with you, not even in long-term relationships."

He raised an eyebrow and Jonas understood what he wanted. What Jonas had said he wanted from Rye. Frankness. "I haven't either," he confessed.

"Well, now, that being the case, I'd like to ask y'all to the saloon yonder for a locally brewed beer." Rye crooked his arm in invitation. "And we can discuss things."

"*Things?*" Jonas would make him work for it.

"Things…like how I've never come so hard, or so many times in one go around." Rye seemed perfectly at ease with the topic. "I swear I nearly fuckin' passed out, man!"

"But you didn't scream," Jonas reminded him. Things…were happening. Rye was no longer some anonymous hookup. He was a real person, interested in Jonas, and in a… Jonas couldn't make himself even think the *R* word. Was he ready for such a thing? Did he want such a thing? He wanted Rye. That he knew. He wanted to be with this man so fiercely he ached with it, even if he didn't understand it. He walked ahead of Rye into the saloon.

"Here do?" Rye placed his hat on a chair and his jacket on its back. "I'll go get us brews." His cell phone rang and he pulled a face. "Sorry. I gotta take that. It's my chief, wanting me to touch base. Won't take a sec." Rye eased his cell free and sauntered to the bar.

He hadn't taken a step before a buzz of a text message sounded...from his jacket pocket. Confused, Jonas had his hand in there before he realized what he was doing. And what he was doing was pulling out an older model cell phone that looked like something from the early 2000s, a device barely able to receive texts, but it must be able to, because that was what the buzz had been, a sound indicating that Rye had received a message.

On what was clearly a burner phone.

All Jonas knew about them was that criminals used them to perform illegal actions, then got rid of them before the cops could trace them.

So why the hell did a lawman, a *Texas Ranger*, have one?

Ideas swarmed through Jonas' head, buzzing and angry like a wasps' nest had been hit by a stick, but he didn't think he wanted any of them confirmed. In fact, he wanted out. Hating that in his neediness, he'd let himself be deceived, he grabbed his briefcase and bolted for the door.

Chapter Eight

It wasn't some instinct that had Rye turning, where he stood at the bar, but more the urge to gaze at Jonas again. He liked looking at the bookish-seeming professor, in that tweed jacket and those black-framed glasses he took off and cleaned about once every sixty seconds...the college teacher who'd understood what Rye craved, and whose commands had taken him apart.

So he turned just in time to see Jonas rushing from the table like his tail was on fire. "Forget those beers," Rye instructed the costumed barkeep he'd just ordered from. He darted back to the table to grab his coat and hat, then raced after Jonas. The guy was not just running out on him but *storming* out? The hell?

"Hey!" he shouted, seeing Jonas a ways along the sidewalk. Jonas must have heard him but didn't turn around or even slow. So Rye sped up. He was used to chasing down his quarry, whether in a vehicle pursuit, a foot chase or even on horseback, and wasn't about to let this one go to ground.

Jonas veered onto a landscaped square, and Rye caught up with him by the bushes at its entrance before Jonas had the chance to lose himself among the food trucks parked along one side of the park or dodge around the café-style tables shaded by umbrellas.

"What the hell fuckin' happened?" Rye demanded. He'd never been known for his subtlety. "Jonas, what's wrong?"

"Your burner phone is what happened, what's wrong. I should be sorry I took it from your pocket to look at what was buzzing, but I'm not." Jonas pulled his shoulder free of Rye's grip and folded his arms across his chest.

Rye slapped his coat pocket. He'd gotten a second cell phone for this trip.

"You got a message," Jonas continued. "A short, three-word message, with the name of a place and the time to be there. You should read it and find the bar, if you don't want to miss your hookup."

"My—?"

"Excuse me."

The woman's irritated voice had Rye breaking off and whipping around, then stepping back to let the young woman push an older one in a wheelchair onto the park. He and Jonas were blocking the entrance. With a muttered, "Sorry, ma'am," he tipped his hat to her.

Jonas had used the break as an excuse to start walking, and, cursing, Rye hurried after him again. "What if I said it ain't what you think?" he tried, speaking to Jonas' back.

Jonas stopped and spun around. "That you're not a player? Not married or in a relationship and hooking up on the downlow? Leading me on, saying you wanted more just to keep me around so you get laid with no effort while you're here?"

"Fuck, no!" Jonas' words appalled Rye. Jonas had delivered them in a cold, hard tone, but that he said them at all spoke volumes. And adding that to the hurt in his eyes and the way he'd reacted earlier when Rye had talked about the two of them exploring what was between them made Rye want to punch out whoever had hurt this man. "I swear."

"Because I thought— Well, it doesn't matter." Jonas shrugged. "But don't worry. I know I mentioned my ideas about the museum, but I won't hang around your place of work like a bunny boiler."

"I want you to hang around." Rye tried to convey his meaning. "I wanna hang around you." That wasn't quite right either and he gritted out a noise of frustration. "Look, let's sit a spell, huh? Looks like we can get coffee here." And it was table service, so Jonas couldn't bolt while Rye was at the kiosk.

The time of day being too late for kids' afternoon playtime on the swings and slides and too early for evening socializing at the dog park, there were a few free tables. Rye chose the one farthest away from the others, on the edge of the area and with some little trees in pots providing cover.

The server hurried over, smiling at Rye, and Rye learned Jonas drank his java black, too. "I ain't no liar," he began. "I meant what I said about not having a second phone to use just for casual sex meet-ups. And I also mean what I say, about wanting to see where things go between us. In which case, I'm more'n happy to be exclusive. Are you?"

Jonas didn't answer. Maybe he didn't know how to, so Rye pushed on. "There's other reasons a fella might have two phones, you know."

"Like celebrities? One for business and one personal?" Jonas flashed back. "Famous singers or actors or sports stars… Should I get your autograph?"

Rye didn't fight the smile crossing his lips. "And what would I be renowned for?"

"You do have a big dick and a sweet ass." Jonas narrowed his eyes as if thinking. "Maybe you're an OnlyFans star."

Rye regretted having taken a mouthful of coffee when he spluttered and near as damn choked on it. When he'd wiped his mouth and streaming eyes, he saw Jonas was busy on his phone. "Don't waste your data looking for BareAss or BigDick Ranger," he advised. "I ain't on that platform or any other. Don't have social media at all. And I don't use a burner phone to buy drugs, if that's what you're thinking."

"No…" Jonas clicked and scrolled. "I'm researching reasons why someone who's not a criminal or a famous person would want a burner phone. The first one that comes up is to avoid roaming charges when you go overseas…"

"Uh-huh and while Texas is big, it ain't that big." Rye nodded. Things were far from going well, but damn if he didn't like spending time with this guy, matching wits in conversation like this. "Any more?"

"Hmm, it says here to get a cheaper old phone if you're going to a dangerous place." Jonas looked up. "It mentions mountaineering or kayaking, or seedy places with a high crime rate, or if you're going to be involved in a possibly violent protest."

Rye looked around the pretty city square. "Can't see no mountains or rivers or opposing factions, can you?"

"You didn't say anything about crime," Jonas said in reply, his voice holding none of the humor that Rye's had.

He's whip smart. Rye had seen that from the off, that Jonas listened harder and watched more closely than most people did, and drew educated conclusions from the information he took in. "Drink your coffee before it gets cold," he said, notching his chin at Jonas.

"I drink quickly. It won't buy you much time," Jonas said, taking a big gulp to prove it.

Despite everything, Rye rasped out a laugh. "Just wait a second," he instructed, indicating the couple pausing fairly near them as their dog wanted to sniff the trees. On another occasion, Rye would have petted the dog, some kind of mastiff — he loved all dogs, the bigger the better — but not today. As soon as the couple had moved off, he dragged his chair nearer to Jonas'.

"I don't need time to think up stories or excuses," he began, making a decision. "I'm gonna tell you what's goin' on. Which means I trust you enough to *tell* you what's going on, okay?" Rye tended to go with his gut. And it was telling him now that he had to level with Jonas, or risk him walking away. That shouldn't matter, seeing as they barely knew each other, and had known each other bare just once, but it did. Rye knew in the marrow of his bones it did.

"And I think you'd know if I was lyin'," he added. "Like I'd, I don't know, touch my earlobe or shuffle my big toe or something."

"I know when you're stallin'," Jonas replied, mimicking the way Rye got extra southern when he was uncomfortable. "Which doesn't mean you're lying, of course. It's more than probable that you're nervous, instead. Hmm. Let me take a guess. What you're going to say is connected to why you're here in San Antonio, isn't it?"

He's good. "Yep. I mean, yes." Rye sat straighter in his chair. "I am here on a temporary assignment, guarding the Waco Hall of Fame items and, well…being a living Texas Ranger, part of the exhibition." He finished in a shrug. He hadn't quite understood that part of things, until today.

"And answering questions from visitors." Jonas had the decency to bite back a smile at the memory.

"Including college professors asking about my crotch." Rye wagged a finger

"Belts!" Jonas protested. "Fine, it's the same general area, but my question was about why Texas Rangers wear two belts. And what you replied, is that the real reason?"

"One for his pants and one for his gun, yeah." Rye grinned. "Least, that's what we're taught at Ranger school. But I'd put up with more, to be able to come here. I need to be in San Antonio and not in Waco right now. I got something I have to do."

He drained half of one of the glasses of water that the server had brought along with their coffees. "I'm gonna ask you to keep everything I'm about to say to yourself, okay?" He waited for Jonas to nod, then continued. "I worked with a partner for about five years, name of Charles Daniels. Chip."

"Work*ed*… What happened to him?" Jonas asked.

"He was killed, right in front of me, when we were on surveillance duty a few nights ago." Rye swallowed and finished his water.

"God. That's *terrible*. I'm so sorry, Rye." Jonas tilted his head to one side, observing him. "But there's more. And it's not good, right?"

"No. It's bad. Least, I think." He found he wanted to pour it all out to Jonas. Maybe Jonas, with his clever, quicker brain, could explain it all away. Or at least give Rye a fresh perspective on it. "Because I think he was dirty."

With his voice a harsh, cracked whisper, his gaze on the table, he listed all the reasons why he suspected Chip was taking kickbacks from the Camargo cartel in exchange for either facilitating or just looking the other way when they transported drugs from South America. He might even have been involved in the cartel's network of stash houses near the border, then distribution centers the deeper into Texas they got.

"His wife — widow — mentioned they'd paid off the mortgage to their property. So I looked it up and yeah, they did. She said they were gonna buy a bigger one...but I found out that Chip already bought another house, earlier this year."

"And you think he used drug money to purchase it?" Jonas asked sharply.

Rye shrugged. "It's a nice place. Owned and rented out to tenants through a company. My thinking is it was his pension pot. He also put down a deposit on a boat. I guess that was his little present to himself. So I thought I'd come here, the place I think the shipment was coming in to Waco from. You probably know that the South Texas border area's the main drug smuggling corridor between the United States and Mexico, and San Antonio's a transshipment center? It's also a place Lina mentioned Chip was spending time in."

"And a specific place was the Lucky Cards Club, I bet. No pun intended." Jonas was silent for a minute or two. "You're investigating this alone, aren't you? It's not part of your secondment here."

Rye nodded. "And if you're wondering why I didn't hand it to my chief—?"

"I'm glad you didn't, with having no real evidence. You'd be accusing someone without proof, and someone who can't defend himself." Jonas snatched his water from the table, and his hand shook a little.

Rye hadn't been expecting that. He'd been prepared to explain that he didn't know who else was involved, but Jonas' anger, because that was how his reaction seemed to Rye, confused him.

"And I know how that feels. What it's like," Jonas continued.

Jonas spoke in such a whisper that Rye had to lean forward to hear him. When he understood, anger and sorrow bloomed like wildflowers in him, and he reached across the table for Jonas' hand. "It's shitty that you went through something like that," he said. "Wish I'd known you then. I'd have—"

"What, snooped around in places you didn't belong and stuck out like a sore lawman? I read your message." Jonas pulled his hand back.

Right. The text must have been from someone who was at the card club, setting up a meet. He should get gone. He didn't know the city very well and he had to find the place. "I gotta do this."

"Alone? It's dangerous!" Jonas looked as horrified at that as he had at Rye accusing his partner. "That place—"

"I gotta go. I'll call you real soon after," Rye promised, getting to his feet. "Everything I said about how I feel about us, about this…" He waved a hand between them. "I meant it." He wanted to drop a kiss on Jonas' head but didn't feel he had the right. So he just winked as he slotted his hat on, then turned and left.

Hot flashes of anger detonated in Jonas and were quickly put out by cold drenches of fear. Rye had promised there was a *this* and an *us*, then marched off to one of the city's most notorious bars, where he'd be spotted as being law enforcement and…dealt with accordingly?

"Not if I can help it," Jonas muttered between clenched teeth.

And luckily for Rye, the bar he was making for this time was another haunt of Jonas'.

Or, rather, of Joe's…

Chapter Nine

Jonas didn't waste any time, just called a rideshare and drove out to the south side of the city where the place Rye had been summoned to was located. Even to an out-of-towner like Rye, unfamiliar with San Antonio, it wouldn't take consulting guidebooks or internet forums to see he was heading out to a bad neighborhood.

Would Rye think it was a cantina or café, by its name? If he did, one look through Nieves Tacos' grimy windows would show him it wasn't a taco bar. It was a bar of sorts, but the main feature was the pool tables, or *tacos*. Jonas had been here a handful of times. It was a good place to pick up the blue-collar types he favored for a night of anonymous sex. He hadn't given a guy his real name, or mentioned what his job was, since he'd turned his back on his 'own sort' — people who'd disowned him when he was falsely accused, and it was made clear to him he should leave the college.

Jonas didn't particularly like pool—he preferred gambling—but he did like the young guys who hung out here. 'Joe' had been with a couple, and they'd been good, dirty encounters. So much so his dick twitched when he saw the flickering neon sign.

Pablo sat in his usual spot just inside the door. On his first visit, Jonas had been wary of the large, muscled dark brown Doberman pinscher, but the highly trained hound barely moved unless told to. He turned his head for his dark eyes to take everything in but didn't even flinch at the loud trash talk before a shot, or the clack of pool balls hitting each other, or the swearing or cheering after a shot.

"But when Pablo gets involved, you should get scared," someone had told Jonas. And true, when Pablo had leaped to his feet once, when some idiot had slammed the butt of his pool stick onto the floor in frustration, everyone present had frozen. But the dog hadn't done anything beyond stare hard in the man's direction, and the guy had raised a hand and muttered an apology.

Jonas paid the entrance fee and walked in. The dry chalk in the air from where players ground the end of their pool sticks into huge squares of it had made his eyes water the first time he was here, but not now. He took a discreet look around the bar section, the easiest part of the place to make out as it was better lit than the column of tables that stretched to the far wall. There were more tables, maybe VIP ones, in recesses to both sides, near the back.

The place was Hispanic, in clientele *and* ownership, he guessed from the name, pointing to the bottled beer to show the woman behind the small wooden counter what he wanted. Who ran this place? Pablo, it seemed, but it was probably the guy who split his time between the door and the bar, overseeing what was going on. He was prowling around now, his gaze hard.

Jonas wasn't naïve. He knew Mexican drug trafficking cartels were a massive problem in the States, dominating illicit drug markets, responsible for most if not all the cocaine entering the country, and that entire law enforcement teams were set up to fight the violence and corruption illegal drugs brought. Rye hadn't been exaggerating or paranoid when he'd sketched the nature of the problem earlier, but the way he was going about it—

A hand on Jonas' arm had him jumping and nearly dropping his beer.

"Woah, Joe, *amigo!*" Luca, the last guy Jonas had hooked up with in here, took a step back, his hands raised. He frowned. "Glasses? And you been for a job interview? Or a court date?" Luca, laughing at his own wit, pointed at Jonas' more formal clothes.

He wore contact lenses and dressed down when trolling for sex but hadn't had the chance to go home and change. "Oh..." He shrugged, taking off his glasses, even though it meant he couldn't see that well. "You know..." Vagueness was a great help at times.

"Come on." Luca led Jonas to one of the nearest tables, where, for form's sake, they became part of the small group watching and betting on the action. The joint was a pickup place, but lip service had to be paid for a minute or two. Jonas contemplated putting money on the heavier-set player. He looked like a winner, like he'd cheat without being detected, to do so. Jonas also tried to search for any sign of Rye.

"So..." With a jerk of his head, Luca steered Jonas into a quiet corner. "What you looking for, *guapo*? Me,

I hope..." He moistened his lips, memories of their couple of nights together shining in his eyes.

The thought of getting with Luca couldn't have been further from Jonas' mind. "I'm not here for anyone," he replied. *Why am I even here?* He had no idea what he was doing, beyond trying to help Rye. "More for some*thing*."

"Go on?" Luca gulped from his beer bottle.

"If I was to say...*coke*, and not the carbonated drink?" Jonas murmured.

Luca shrugged, looking only mildly surprised. "Sure. I can get you some."

"Right now? In here?" Jonas pressed.

Luca nodded.

"Good stuff? From over the border?"

"*Si*," Luca replied, trying to appear casual, but the sudden stilling of his body gave away his tension.

"Camargo cartel stuff?" Jonas asked, feeling like a scientist making a breakthrough when Luca's shaking his thick dark hair from his eyes, his tell, told Jonas what he needed to know. "This is their place, right?"

"*Hombre...*" Luca widened his eyes and brought a forefinger to his lips in the classic *shh* gesture.

"This place." Jonas lowered his voice even more, although it was probably unnecessary given the increased volume of noise from somewhere down the end of the pool room. "Is it a deposit?" No, that wasn't the right term! He tried to think above the *thump thump* of his heart in his ears. "A depot. An intermediate locale. A transshipment center."

Luca twitched his head, as if to flick his hair into place.

Shit. That last term had been the correct one. Things seemed so unreal, so quickly, that a part of Jonas dissociated from the here and now, feeling instead like he was taking part in some game show where he had to guess the right word. He dragged in a breath. *Okay, so the bar's a place in which cocaine and — There're more drugs than just cocaine.* "Am I in the right place for amphetamines too?" he asked, going for broke.

"Joe. *Cállate la boca.*" Luca took a tiny glance around, checking if anyone had heard him telling Jonas to shut his mouth. He leaned his top half closer, his lower half pointing away, distancing himself. "You being here for like, I don't know, slum sex, that's one thing. But this...*esto es una mierda seria. Mierda mortal, sabes*?" He hissed the final word.

Jonas agreed. It *was* serious. Deadly even.

"Get out," Luca advised, jerking his head toward the door.

He stopped when the woman came out from behind the bar. She threw them a look from her hard black eyes but didn't stop by them. She marched past and beckoned the man Jonas had thought was the manager or overseer to her. The jerkiness, the urgency of her actions caught Jonas' attention, and he rammed on his glasses to look where she was pointing. He just knew it was Rye—

—bursting backward out of one of the far alcoves, fighting two men at the same time. *Shit. Shit!* He'd been there all this time, probably asking questions and—no, been lured there, to see what he knew.

"*Sal!*" urged Luca, telling Jonas, not for the first time, to get out.

And leave Rye? Rye who was taking hits as well as delivering them, in a place full of enemies, with weapons? Metal flashed in the guys' hands, small and curved, not like blades as much as talons. Jonas didn't understand what they were and didn't want a closer look. And that big dog could be sent in any minute! When he hesitated, Luca grabbed him and heaved him bodily from the bar, shoving him out onto the street then went back in.

"You were never here!" he called over his shoulder as he vanished, yanking the door closed behind him.

"But I am!" Jonas yelled back stupidly. He took a deep breath and yelled *"Policias!"* but not as if calling the police for help. He made his voice a warning and banged a fist on the grimy window. *"Policias estan llegando!"*

A passerby scoffed. "Cops don't come here," he said in English.

Oh no? There was one inside. *"Policias!"* Jonas shouted again, desperate now, then stumbled back onto the sidewalk when the door opened again — and Rye was pushed out. He turned, as if to force his way in again, but the door was slammed shut.

"Rye?"

Rye whirled around at Jonas' gasp, and Jonas almost vomited. Rye's face was bleeding, although Jonas couldn't see where the blood was coming from in the mess.

"Not here," Rye said, wiping his mouth with the back of one hand and checking out both sides of the street before pulling Jonas away.

Jonas could barely contain himself as they hurried around a corner. "How could you be so stupid? I told you what would happen if you went there! That you'd stand out, attract attention — it was obvious!" he half-yelled.

"So you think I'm stupid. Well, ain't that the type you like, working-class guys who go to places like that?" Rye shouted back. "Or maybe I should have gone in disguise, taken another name, so no one in these kinda dives where I go to trawl for a quick fuck knows who I really fuckin' am?"

"How dare you." Jonas almost shook with his anger. "You don't know — you don't understand —"

"I guess I don't. But I'd like to."

"*Here? Now?*" Jonas wondered if Rye was ridiculing him. No. Rye wasn't the sort. Could it be he'd heard Jonas addressed as *Joe* here too, or seen that he was if not a regular there, that he'd been there before? He had a right to be curious. He was clearly angry Jonas had been there tonight, was a part of this mess.

Rye was waiting, so Jonas shrugged. "Yes, I went after you. To protect you."

"Which you didn't need to do." Rye scowled. "But it wasn't your first time there. In places like that."

Jonas shook his head then nodded. Seeing a fight like that, from a ringside view, would have thrown most people. It being Rye in the thick of it, outnumbered, outgunned... Reaction was setting in and making Jonas weak and trembly. He fought it and tried to focus on what Rye had asked. That was a big thing too.

"It's not some ghetto or barrio fixation. Neither is it curiosity or for kicks.," he started. "It's that, well, every relationship I had got severed when I was accused of something I didn't do, and it was easier for people and the institution to jettison me than stand by me and fight it. *Every* relationship, including that with the guy I'd been with for over two years, and whom I believed loved me. So that world...now...I can't." He exhaled. This was hard. "I suppose I find blue-collar guys more honest..."

"Yeah, if you don't understand it properly, I'm not gonna. But now it's your turn to try to understand that I ain't stupid," Rye replied.

Jonas raised an eyebrow, trailing his gaze down Rye's injuries.

"Oh, so you think I can't handle myself? I'm a goddamn Texas Ranger!" Rye protested. "That?" He jerked a thumb back at the bar. "That coulda been a lot fuckin' worse. *I* could have dished out a lot fuckin' worse."

"So you let them do this?" Jonas' eyes bugged out of his head at Rye's bloody face. "*Why?*"

"It's like...an opening," Rye explained. "The first step."

"It's hardly ballroom dancing," Jonas protested, relief that Rye was still walking and talking coursing through him. "Like an opening gambit in chess?"

"I wouldn't know. Maybe?" Rye shrugged. "Here's my ride." He fumbled for his keys, winced, and his jacket fell open.

Jonas gasped.

Shit. Rye would have preferred Jonas didn't see that. Would definitely have preferred Jonas not twitch Rye's jacket open farther, to see the mess under it, his shirt shredded down his torso and lines of blood oozing through tears in his skin, visible in each rip.

"*Rye?* You were *stabbed?*" Jonas' voice rose in pitch with each word, and his knees buckled.

Chapter Ten

"*Scratched.* I was scratched," Rye corrected, grabbing for Jonas' arm when he sagged, hating how pale Jonas had gone.

"Deep scratched," Jonas whispered, a hand going to his mouth. "Many scratched. Those curved metal things that those bastards had on their hands... They looked like talons, but I couldn't see so I thought they were brass knuckles, but they were *knives*?"

The lion's paw weapon, metal that fitted over the wrist and fingers and had claws coming out of the end, was technically a many-bladed dagger, designed to slash through skin and muscle and even an organ if the user was strong and skilled enough, but Jonas didn't need to know that. He was babbling enough already.

"It's just a flesh wound, but I'll feel better once it's cleaned," Rye admitted. "So let's go? You in your car?"

"No. I'm in your oversized sold-as-a-truck-but-it's-almost-a-tank truck, and I'm driving," Jonas retorted and before Rye understood what he meant or what was happening, Jonas had snatched the keys and was in the driver's seat of Rye's Ford, leaving Rye no option but to scramble in after him.

He was kind of glad that Jonas was doing the work, even if it meant listening to him bitch all the way about why anyone who wasn't a farmer, or a rancher, needed a truck and how much did Rye have to tow or haul in the city and how much horsepower did he need and what was that a compensation for?

"Most sold pickup truck in America," Rye observed. "You telling me all those people are wrong? And the cubic capacity and gas mileage you get with the F150 is great." That they were bickering like a long-standing couple made him smile — despite the discomfort he was in — just like their banter had earlier. It took him a while to notice they weren't headed to his motel. In his defense, he didn't know the city that well.

"You're not taking me to the hospital?" he asked, disbelief in his voice.

"No." Jonas seemed to be taking them back to the museum. No — they left downtown for midtown.

"But not my motel."

"You said you wanted your injury cleaned." Jonas turned off into a residential street of small houses. "Clean isn't the first adjective that comes to mind about the place you're staying in, and does the room have a first aid kit?"

Probably not, but he did. He'd let Jonas minister to him though. It had been a while since anyone had.

"We're here." Jonas cut the engine and indicated the one-story.

"Jonas —" Rye stopped him getting out. "Sorry. And thank you." He knew what he meant. He hoped Jonas did.

Jonas nodded. His color had come back. "Good idea to thank me now, before you've experienced my lack of medical skills," he replied. "I'm pretty sure you won't after."

"Bet I will," Rye told him. "And what I'm sorry for is that you were a witness to that. It's not your problem. Not your fight. You didn't need to."

"Except it is and yes I do, because I care about you," Jonas interrupted. He looked surprised by what he'd said.

His frankness caught Rye by surprise as well. "I care about you too. I know, it's crazy, seeing how we only just met and—"

"And you're bleeding all over your nice tank. Come on."

Inside, Rye took in the wooden bookshelves and framed artwork everywhere. "*This* is nice," he commented. "Looks like a real professor's place."

"It is. He's on sabbatical and I'm subletting from him." Jonas nudged Rye down a short corridor to a small utility room off the kitchen. "I know there's a first aid box in there. Take your shirt off and sit down. And yes, it's not the first time I've said that."

"Wouldn't that be 'and lie down'?" Rye called after him, doing as he'd been told and taking a seat at the small, narrow breakfast-type table. "I liked this shirt," he muttered, dabbing at the cuts with the ruined cotton cloth. The gouges weren't that deep, and they'd mostly stopped bleeding.

His eyes widened at the size of the white plastic box Jonas brought in. "He a little accident-prone, this prof? Or he like to be prepared?"

"The former. And his wife, the latter." Jonas set the box down, cleaned his glasses then scrubbed his hands at the faucet. "You realize I have no idea what I'm doing, beyond what I've seen in movies?"

"Long as you don't give me a strip of leather to bite on while you dig the bullet out, we're golden," Rye started, then stopped on seeing Jonas' expression. "Joke! There weren't no bullets."

"There could have been." Jonas' movements were jerky as he sat opposite and ripped some cotton wool from the roll inside the kit.

Rye silently debated if he should explain again that the encounter at the pool hall had been a move, on both parties' sides, and not intended as a showdown. No, it wouldn't do any good revisiting the scene now, and especially seeing as he'd learned nothing there. He'd have to wait, see if they responded to his lure, or dig somewhere else. Jonas didn't need to be reminded of what he'd witnessed.

Normally, it was the guy getting tended to who needed to be distracted with chitchat while the medic worked, but here, the roles were reversed, Rye saw. Kind of like earlier, with Jonas thinking to rush to Rye's rescue. "Where's the prof you're letting from gone to? And is his wife at the college as well?" he asked.

"Canada. And no, she's a painter." Jonas told him a few more details about the couple and their work while pressing on the wounds to stop any last bleeding, then cleaning them and Rye's face with antiseptic wipes. He breathed out a laugh. "You know, in movies, when the tough guy goes through hell, he takes it all on the chin without a murmur, then winces and grimaces when someone cleans him up afterward?"

"Movies versus real life, I guess. Like how puttin' on a cape don't mean you can fly?" Rye replied. He could have done the doctoring himself, but was happy to have Jonas' hands on him, especially the way he took his time pressing gauze on Rye's chest to dry off the antiseptic, then slowly smeared an antibiotic ointment along the red marks. He was leaning close, close enough for Rye to notice he had a couple of freckles near his nose and catch a faint lemon scent of cologne or soap.

Rye wrapped his fingers around Jonas' wrist, when he finished, stilling his hand before Jonas could move away. "Thanks. Best doctor I ever had. But you forgot the final step."

"I did? What?" Jonas asked.

"Kissing me better."

They hadn't kissed yet. Done plenty of other stuff, but not kissed. So now, Rye leaned forward a little and angled his head to one side. Jonas copied him, their movements two halves of a whole, and their lips met. Met slowly, softly, but the touch sent a quiver through Rye. He thought he was the one to initiate the brush of his tongue against Jonas', but it didn't matter.

Jonas eased back and studied him. "Crazy..." He repeated Rye's word of before, a way to describe things between them, the speed, the intensity. "And I don't do relationships." He said it like he was tasting a sour candy. "But this..."

"*This*." It was Rye's turn to echo, and he cupped Jonas' face for them to gaze into each other's eyes.

"What?" Jonas asked, suspicion in his voice.

"What what?" Rye replied.

"The look in your eye," Jonas explained. "Intense. Heated."

"Oh yeah." Rye stood, drawing Jonas with him and helping him round the table. "It would be, when I want you inside me, your cock filling me. I don't know what you do to me or what this is between us but—"

Maybe Jonas did. He pushed Rye, who landed against the kitchen counter at his back, his hands flying either side of him to grip it and his mouth opening on a gasp. That must have been Jonas' intention, because he moved on Rye, kissing him again and this time leaving soft and slow and gentle behind. Now his moves were dirty, him plunging his tongue in and staking his claim, cupping Rye's ass and squeezing.

Rye was hard within seconds, his body as heated as Jonas had said. Jonas broke off the kiss, leaving Rye gasping, and moved his lips to Rye's lower neck where he sucked and nibbled at the mark he'd left yesterday. Goosebumps broke out all over Rye's body. "*Damn*," he ground out.

"Come on." Jonas took his hand and went to lead him, but Rye tugged him back for another one of those kisses first. God if he wasn't addicted to them. He let Jonas lead him after that, down the corridor and to the bedroom.

"Let me," Jonas said, when Rye went to unfasten his jeans. But Jonas didn't undo them right away, instead cupping the bulge tenting them. Maybe because he was too mindful of Rye's cuts to pinch or bite his nipples, and he needed another playground?

"Was so fucking hot, you playing with my nipples," Rye admitted. "I didn't even know I was into that, but I think I could come from your teeth on them alone."

If he was trying to take control, to set the pace, it didn't work. Jonas pushed him again and this time Rye landed on the bed, Jonas following him down and straddling him. Rye pressed into the friction. "Love your dick. Wanna ride you all fuckin' night," he muttered, watching Jonas take condoms and lube…and other things from the nightstand drawer.

Jonas' eyes were so dark brown they looked black when he stared into Rye's. "If you only knew the things I want to do to you."

"Tell me," Rye urged.

Jonas smiled. "I'll show you." He sat up, kneeling between Rye's legs, and popped open the top button on his jeans. He slid the zipper down slowly, then, more slowly still, palmed the black cotton of the briefs Rye wore underneath, cupping him again through the material. "I like these."

"Yeah, I see that," Rye managed to say, before Jonas' tap had him lifting up for Jonas to remove his jeans—but not his briefs. His cock strained against the fabric, more so once Jonas focused in on that area. Jonas pausing, just looking, had Rye ready to hump the air, so when Jonas eventually lowered himself and buried his face in Rye's groin, Rye had to work hard not to yell.

And Jonas licking his cock through the briefs made Rye cry out. How did the touch of Jonas' tongue through tight cotton, fabric he left heated and damp behind him, feel so fucking amazing? Rye was still processing that when Jonas stripped the underwear from him, lifted Rye's cock and took half his length into his mouth.

"Oh God." Rye's hips bucked. "Jonas, please. Stop. Let me see you too." He flapped a hand, trying to show Jonas that he wanted him naked as well. He might be disrupting Jonas' plans, breaking the flow of whatever Jonas had in mind, but he needed to see him.

After a second's hesitation, Jonas backed off the bed and stripped. Jesus, his body was hot. Well, Rye knew that, but seeing it, he *knew* it. The dark fuzz on Jonas' chest had Rye aching to scratch his fingernails through it. He propped himself up, leaning on his elbows, so when Jonas returned to the bed, kneeling astride him, Rye was in the perfect position to get a good view of his dick, thick and long and glistening at the tip.

The position Rye was in wasn't ideal, but he arched, desperate to get a taste and no sooner had he snaked out his tongue than Jonas thrust, forcing his broad cockhead into Rye's mouth. Rye took in as much as he could, as far to the back of his throat as he could manage. Or, more accurately, as Jonas allowed, before he slid free.

"Move," he ordered, and it took an impatient flick of his finger for Rye to understand. But when he did, he turned around and lay on his side, for Jonas to mirror his action, lying alongside him, his head level with Rye's dick, and pressed a slicked finger into Rye's ass.

When had he gotten at the lube? Rye didn't know and couldn't spare any time to think, not when Jonas slid a second finger into his ass at the same time as he eased his cock into Rye's mouth then thrust, pulling back, sliding in, working his cock and fingers in tempo, penetrating Rye with both harder and deeper each stroke.

Shit. All Rye could do was grip the base of Jonas' erect cock and take as much as he could in his mouth. His attempt faltered when Jonas increased his suction and pushed his fingers deeper inside his hole, sending jolts of elec-fucking-tricity through him. Jonas wriggled his fingers and flickered his tongue, and the jolts became volts, shorting out every nerve end in Rye's body, the pleasure on the edge of pain...his favorite place.

Rye rode the fingers in his ass—Jesus, were there three now? And Jonas didn't exactly have slim, delicate hands—trying to take Jonas' dick deep. Jonas pressed his evening stubble into Rye's skin, making him squirm and buck, which made him thrust deeper, and Jonas suck harder.

"Jesus, fuck!" Rye had to slide his mouth free to exclaim, when Jonas rubbed the tip of his tongue against that extra sensitive spot just under the head of Rye's dick, making him release so much pre-cum it was halfway to cum.

Jonas stopped too and pinched Rye's thigh to get him to look, and when Rye did, the sight of Jonas sticking out his tongue that was coated in Rye had Rye's hips thrusting. It was obscene and filthy and beautiful. And so skilled, Rye couldn't emulate it. All he could do was spread what he'd coaxed from the head of Jonas' dick along his length to jack him root to tip while cradling his high, hard balls with his other hand. This meant he didn't have to deep-throat, just play with the tip of Jonas' cockhead.

He felt pride at making Jonas writhe, even if he didn't falter in his rhythm on Rye's cock. If anything, it had him upping his game, rubbing over Rye's prostate every other stroke, a move that had Rye howling and shaking the tears from his eyes. Then Jonas pressed harder than he had yet on that gland and licked over the throbbing vein that ran from the base of Rye's shaft to just under the head, and Rye started to explode in a burst of pure bright-lightning sensation. All he could do for Jonas was plunge his mouth down his dick in one last long, hard suck.

It seemed to be the right move. It made Jonas moan around Rye's dick, the vibrations sending more prickles down Rye's spine and into his balls, and he surrendered to the blinding climax Jonas demanded of him and in which Jonas joined him, pulsing in Rye's mouth. Rye joyfully swallowed down Jonas' release, fighting to hold Jonas' hips against the bed when he thrust too forcefully as he spasmed. He made sure he held Jonas in his mouth until he'd wrung the last drop from him, and his body finally relaxed.

"Holy shit. Jesus fuck," Rye gasped, subsiding onto his back and clinging to Jonas' leg, which was all he could reach. And even that was denied him when Jonas moved. But only for a second — Jonas pushed himself around to lie the right way round with Rye. He didn't hold him close, pull him into his arms, but Rye felt this was something Jonas didn't often or easily do.

Their hands touched, then clasped, and Jonas twisted to look at him. "You okay?" he asked.

"Fucking A," Rye replied immediately. "You?"

"Fucking A too." Jonas laughed. "That reminds me of grading papers. Fucking A sounds like it should be a category."

He looked younger and lighter in his mirth, and Rye loved seeing him like that. He laughed too, stopping when it pulled on his chest wounds. "It's okay," he assured Jonas. "Seeing you laugh makes the whole evening worth it. Well, and the fuckin' A-plus sex too. Makes up for the crap that went down in the pool bar and being no further along."

"But we are," Jonas said slowly. "You were right, not only about the cartel running the distribution of cocaine from the border into Texas, but the supply route too. I found out."

All Rye could do was stare at him.

Chapter Eleven

I'm in a relationship. This…is a relationship. Jonas blinked at the realization. The admission. He'd sworn he wouldn't do that, after what had happened with Ben, which was far from the only shitty relationship he'd been in. But this…had happened. Was happening. But wasn't it too soon to call it that? It had only been a handful of days. Jonas stood, the bustle and noise of the museum all around him, lost in thought.

He tried to be academic about things, to analyze the material. In the *No, it can't be* column was the fact that it had only been two days after he'd brought Rye back to his place to spend the night. In the *Maybe it is?* column was that they'd been pretty much inseparable since, spending every night together, mostly at Jonas', and only really parting when Jonas had to be at the university. The department was somewhere he was basically straight in and out to fulfill his teaching duties, with most of his time spent at the downtown museum.

Like now, when he should be sitting in a quiet corner, reading through and taking notes from the old letters and diaries. Well, he was doing that, and the material was sparking off a whole lot of ideas and thoughts in him, and not just for how to use the items as objects in museum studies. Or it would be more accurate to say he had been doing that, and was now on his feet, watching and listening to Rye interact with the guide and the museum visitors.

"Mister! Can I try on your hat?" called one schoolkid.

"Mister Ranger, sir, can I see your badge?" another begged.

There'd been field trips or families in every day, and Rye charmed them all. He had a niece and nephew, he'd told Jonas, and most of his co-workers had kids. Rye's answers to questions about Texas Rangers had painted a picture of his background for Jonas, and in return, he'd described his fascination with American history to Rye, who shared a lot of his interests. Jonas felt he knew Rye better than he did most, if not all, of his colleagues in the department, even after such a short time together.

Rye was getting to know him too, and some of the facets to Jonas astounded him.

"What, y'all can't cook at all?" he'd repeated amazed, when Jonas had ordered in again last night, this time Korean food.

"It's never interested me. And why bother, when anything you could ever want is readily available?" Jonas had tried to sound lofty, even under Rye's skeptical eye. "In buying readymade food, I'm creating employment for an entire sector of the economy."

Rye had raised an eyebrow at that, making Jonas admit, "Fine. I'm just clueless in the kitchen. I wouldn't have any idea where to start."

"Oh, that's easy. Y'all start with the basics," Rye had replied.

Earlier that morning, he'd shown Jonas what he meant. Jonas smiled, reliving the scene. He was far from being a morning person, but he thought Rye, in his kitchen, shirtless and with an apron tied around his waist, might get him out of bed early. No, Rye shirtless would make him — preferably them — get out of bed late.

Narrow-eyed, he raised a warning finger. "There'd better be —"

"Coffee?" Rye handed him a mug.

Jonas sniffed it. Good and strong.

"Should wake you up enough to find your glasses." Rye imitated Jonas' squint. "You'll need them to see what I'm doing."

"And that would be...?" Jonas brushed Rye aside to take a spare pair from the kitchen drawer. Life was so much easier with multiple pairs of glasses stashed everywhere.

"Teaching you how to cook. Starting with my never-fail beginner-level grilled cheese." Rye brandished a breadknife.

"What? A sandwich isn't *cooking*!" Jonas protested.

"Wait till you taste it. Okay, ready? Now, I went out and got this thick-sliced Texas toast bread and unsalted butter." He held them up.

Jonas spluttered out coffee. "Rye, are you filming content for some kind of sexy shirtless Texas Ranger cooking channel?" he asked when he'd finished choking.

"Oh, think I'm sexy, do ya?" Rye winked. "And good try, but I ain't stopping the lesson. So, now let's soften the butter…"

Despite himself, Jonas watched rapt, although that was probably more to do with the chef than the food.

"Jonas…" Rye paused in his sauteing or browning. "Are you taking *notes*?"

"Oh, am I?" He'd automatically reached for a pad and pen. "I am, yes. And I have questions."

"*Questions?*" It was Rye's turn to splutter. "It's *grilled cheese* — you can't have questions about grilled cheese!"

Jonas dodged the dish towel Rye snapped at him. "I do, actually, starting with why do you keep saying grilled when you're not grilling it?" He pointed at the skillet on the stove, where Rye was flipping the sandwich over.

"You *can* grill it." Rye seemed serious as he answered. "But you'd wanna keep the heat very low to not burn your bread before the cheese melts."

"I see." Jonas scribbled a note, then flipped the page. "Now, second question. The bread —" This time he failed to dodge the slap to his ass. "Hey! I have questions about the type of cheese too!" He held up his page as proof.

"Just eat it." Rye sliced the golden-brown sandwich and set it on a plate, pulling out a chair for Jonas. "What? What now?" he asked when Jonas hesitated, forehead furrowed.

"Why do you cut it on the diagonal like that?" Jonas pointed at the plate.

"Hell if I know! It tastes better?" Rye exclaimed. He poured more coffee.

Jonas took a bite. "Oh my," he said thickly, round the mouthful of melting salty cheese and crisp buttery toast. "I mean, oh *my*." He bit off another huge chunk at once.

"Told ya." Rye smiled smugly.

"Where's yours?" Jonas pointed from the plate to Rye and raised his shoulders and hands to make his question understandable—he was speaking with his mouth full.

"Mine? There." Rye slapped the packet of bread and flicked the slices of cheese. "And you're gonna make it for me. Don't look at me like that. I thought you were a big fan of all that hands-on, experimental learning?"

So Jonas tried, and Rye reached over his shoulder only once, to turn the heat down when Jonas whacked it up, to cook quicker, and it wasn't...that bad. Rye praised him as he ate it, anyway, making Jonas glow inside. He served Rye more coffee and sat next to him, his chair dragged close enough that their bodies touched all down one side.

"Next step, maybe for a lunch or supper, I'll show you my famous Texas cheesesteak." Rye chugged half his mug of coffee in one mouthful. "Also known as a cowboys' cheesesteak."

"Isn't it a *Philly* cheesesteak?" Jonas asked.

"*What?* And you call yourself a good Texan?" Rye looked horrified.

It was the most fun and warmth Jonas had had or felt in a good long time, but he was a realist. Things weren't this easy. He took in a breath. "Are we going to discuss the elephant in the room?"

"The—?"

"Why you're here," Jonas broke in, not wanting Rye to look around or feel dumb. "The drugs distribution route. The cartel. Corruption." He hated to do this, but they couldn't ignore the very real problem. "What's your next move?"

Rye gave a slow shake of his head, his lips compressed. "I don't reckon I can do more right at this moment, you know? I can't exactly go bustin' down doors or crackin' skulls. I'll give 'em a little longer to contact me, see how that moves things forward."

"And if they don't?" Jonas selfishly hoped they didn't. The injuries to Rye's torso hadn't been more than deep scratches, as he'd said, and his face had cleaned up fine, but still.

"Then I'll have to go back and place this higher up the chain. Yeah, I don't know who's dirty." He anticipated Jonas' next objection. "But I'll write the case up—"

"Write your suspicions up," Jonas couldn't help muttering.

"Yeah." Rye pulled a face, showing what his treatment of his partner was costing him. "And send it to everyone above me in the chain of command."

Jonas, a gambler, understood that strategy and nodded. "Percentage play. They can't all be involved." He thought for a second. "But couldn't you get around that by handing this over, not up? To the FBI or whichever national agency is tasked with narcotics or organized crime?" He'd been pondering that, but Rye's reaction told him he'd touched a nerve. "You think it'd be admitting that you can't handle it, when you prefer to deal with things alone? You don't trust other people?"

Rye stood with a jerk and took their dishes to the sink, placing them in with a clatter. "I'd be saying the Texas Rangers couldn't handle it. Which ain't the case. And no one in any other agency knew Chip. They wouldn't understand the guy he was or why... They'd treat him like some criminal. I mean, like any other criminal." He shrugged.

Jonas thought he understood. Rye's reasons for doing what he was doing, for dealing with things in this single-handed way, were myriad and complex, shaped by what he'd been through in life. If anyone could understand that, it should be Jonas. And that Rye wanted to protect his partner's reputation as much as possible humbled Jonas.

"But if you're worried that you're involved, don't be." Rye turned to him.

Jonas shook his head. They didn't need to go through that again, that Jonas going by Joe in that world, and never having divulged his real name or any details of his life, meant there was no connection to the very proper Professor Jonas Abrams of Laurel Heights University. They both took their own cars to the museum, or to Jonas' or Rye's, and Rye insisted they took different routes each trip too.

All that played in Jonas' head as he stood watching Rye help the guide show the items, and the fact that someone was trying to attract his attention didn't register until he felt a hand on his arm. He yanked free and whirled around, twisting to the side that the touch had come from and bringing his other arm up in defense.

"*Jonas?*" Aldric sounded shocked, as well he might.

"Aldric, I'm so sorry!" Jonas hated to see that look of shock in his younger co-worker's big brown eyes. It took him back to his—and Aldric's—earliest days at Intrinsic Value, when getting caught up in a crime of greed that had turned violent had shaken the shy, unsure young Aldric to the core.

"No, it's my fault." Aldric had his hand over his mouth in a way he hadn't for a while now. "You were absorbed in your work, and I startled you." He started to back away—and thudded into Darrell.

"Everything all right?" The taller, broader and more stolid Darrell Williams slid to the side of Aldric and moved his hazel-eyed gaze from him to Jonas.

"Of course." Jonas tried on a smile.

"Told you it might not be a good idea to disturb Jonas at work!" Darrell removed any sting from his rebuke of Aldric by ruffling his fluffy dark hair.

"But we never see him!" Aldric protested. "You're always here these days! So I thought the place must be really good if you're spending all your time here." Bratty triumph laced his words.

"The new *exhibition* must be good," Darrell corrected, looking around at it. "It's not just that you helped set it up—although it looks great—but that you're trying to put something together from it or use it as an example, right?"

"Oh, in the idea for a new course to present to your department!" Aldric finished his partner's speech for him, showing their closeness.

They must have discussed Jonas' phone call to Darrell for a morale boost, and the pep talk Darrell had tried to give. Jonas loved that degree of complicity the couple enjoyed. He also appreciated the fact that even though they didn't fully understand what he was trying to do in his career, they were supportive of him. Elliot and Drew were too.

"And Darrell wanted to come see the things," Aldric finished, in a sneaky mutter.

"Brat," Darrell replied. "But you're doing okay, Jonas?"

"Oh, I'm fine, thanks. Yes, caught up here and…" He gestured.

"There a problem?" Rye interrupted, suddenly in their midst. He moved to Jonas' side, like Darrell stood at Aldric's, his stance protective and his narrow-eyed gaze raking Aldric and Darrell. "Jonas?"

Jonas sought for words, but Aldric got in first. "I'm Aldric Beamer."

"Oh, from the store? Howdy." Rye held out a hand. "Gabe Ryland. Which makes you…Darren? No—that's not it…"

"Sergeant Darrell Williams," Aldric said, bursting with pride as Darrell and Rye shook hands. He slid his gaze over Rye and Jonas and sly understanding crossed his sweet-looking face, replaced within seconds by frank curiosity, then regret. "Shoot. I have to get to class."

"I can drive—"

"Stay and talk," Aldric cut Darrell's offer off with a thinly disguised order.

The pushy little thing wants information! Aldric confirmed Jonas' supposition when he elbowed Darrell and jerked his head toward Rye as he said goodbye and left.

"So, Field Ranger Ryland," Darrell began a little awkwardly.

"Darrell's with the San Antonio Police Department," Jonas said, an idea forming.

"Guessed that." Rye looked back at the guide. "There's some local TV show people coming to film, and I have to be on hand to guarantee the safety of the loan items. Excuse me."

"So…"

Darrell's equivalent of a fake cough recalled Jonas to where he was—staring at Rye as he rejoined the guide and staff. "So," Darrell continued. "You can't take your eyes off him and he's very protective of you…anything you want to tell us?"

Jonas suddenly found there was. And not anything—*everything*. "Could I confide in you?" he asked in a whisper and at Darrell's surprised nod, led him to a small storeroom, where he locked the door and before Darrell could react and before he himself lost his nerve, launched into the tale of what had really brought Rye to San Antonio.

The long exhale Darrell gave at the end was almost a whistle.

"So it's not just that he feels his partner was involved in the cocaine distribution route—he fears actions by their superiors led to this man's death. That his partner was a pawn they sacrificed." Jonas was figuring out Rye's tangle of emotions as he spoke.

Darrell gave a slow nod, telling Jonas he was working through the information dump Jonas had laid on him.

"Do you know anything that can help?" Jonas asked.

"*Me?*" Darrell looked shocked. "It's not my area at all. But I guess I can ask discreetly. Carefully. But it's you I'm worried about!"

"I'm fine," Jonas protested. "No one knows who I am. No one knows Rye and I are…" *Whatever we are.*

"You only have to see you together to know!" Darrell exclaimed. "Jonas, do you carry a gun?" He grimaced at Jonas' head shake. "I'll give you one and make sure you know how to use it. Right now. This evening while the Ranger's working. Come on. And one more thing."

Jonas could see he'd like this even less and braced himself.

"I'm also giving the pair of you forty-eight hours to make a break in the case…then I'm calling it in."

Chapter Twelve

Jonas was glad he was working nonstop the day after that, both at his teaching and admin duties and the target practice Darrell insisted on—it stopped him missing Rye too much when Rye was busy, checking out an airfield and digging into who owned the cards club and the pool hall. Jonas barely remembered Rye arriving home—he'd given Rye a spare key—but was glad he'd come. He liked having Rye in his bed, his big, solid body wound around his own, holding him close.

He remembered dropping off to sleep with Rye's heat warming his back, and his fingers stroking Jonas' hand. And now Jonas had woken slightly less gently than he'd fallen asleep...because Rye was stroking a very different part of Jonas' body.

"What are you doing?" he asked.

Rye twisted to look at him but didn't stop. "What does it feel like?"

"Like—" Jonas' breath tangled in his throat when Rye rubbed his thumb over the tip of his cock. "Like *that*." He pushed into Rye's grip.

"Hey, don't go blaming me when you're the one who woke up hard for me. I'm just helping you take the pressure off," Rye told him.

"So...*ah*...noble," Jonas teased back. "Selfless. Because there's nothing in this for you, of course." He was amazed he was even that coherent, with Rye's callused hand working him from base to head.

"Oh...how about you return the favor after?" Rye asked.

"After...?" Jonas opened his eyes to look at him, but Rye wasn't there. He was ducking under the sheet and slipping lower and the next second, Jonas' breath left him on a long gasp when Rye's mouth engulfed his dick in wet warmth. Jonas almost choked when Rye teased his tongue tip along the crown and cupped Jonas' balls.

"Oh, *after*," Jonas sighed in understanding, twisting so he was flat on his back, then widening the space between his legs to give Rye room to work. He twitched the sheet away to enjoy the sight. And it was one glorious view to behold. He didn't usually let a partner lead, but it was just one thing in the list of things he was doing with Rye that—

"*Jesus!*" Jonas' body jackknifed and he almost hit Rye in the face. "Are you *humming*?" he managed. No one had ever gotten him this hard and this close to the edge so quickly.

Rye's answer was something approaching a chuckle, and he rolled Jonas' balls in his palm, tugging as he worked him quicker.

"Rye, I'm—" Jonas tried to warn him, but it only made Rye vibrate his throat around him tighter and squeeze his balls harder, making everything in Jonas blazing hot and coiled tight before it released and he came, swept helplessly along on the blinding white tide of his orgasm.

"Rye," Jonas panted, as soon as he could, when he was back in his body, and his mind—it felt like he'd left them. "Rye, come up here."

He pulled and Rye pushed until they were close again. "That…" Jonas tried but finished in a shrug.

"That," Rye agreed. "I'd kiss ya good morning but…" He wiped his mouth. His lips were wet, shiny and a little swollen and the head of his hard cock slick as he rubbed against Jonas' thigh.

"Move a little," Jonas ordered, getting Rye into position. If Rye thought he was calling the shots, directing play, he had another think coming. He paused, keeping Rye on the edge, flushed and throbbing, before curling into him and taking him in his hand. He pressed close, making sure to drag his coarse body hair over Rye's full balls, and waited until he heard Rye whimper out his need.

Then Jonas buried his face in Rye's neck, giving teasing nips with his lips and teeth before biting down. This was the opposite side to where he'd bitten before, and Rye would wear a matching mark. Jonas increased the pressure of the bite along with the speed and constriction of his hand, jacking Rye from root to tip.

When Rye squirmed, trying to thrust or arch, Jonas held him down with knees and elbows, making Rye his prisoner. "Next time I'll tie you down," he breathed into Rye's ears, his words a dark velvet promise, one that had Rye bringing his free hand up to scratch his nails down Jonas back.

"Naughty…" Jonas whispered, before biting down harder and making his hand a firm band at the base of Rye's dick, enjoying the hot pulse and kick of it in his hand, then how each pass made it slicker, the tip sticky with pre-cum.

He brought Rye to the edge until he was a whimpering, writhing mess of desperation—then stopped. He loosened the grip of his hand and turned his mouthing at Rye's neck into a soft kiss of his lips, counting how long it took Rye to thrust into nothing and beg Jonas to bring him relief.

Jonas did, adding rubbing his chest hair over Rye's nipples to his biting and jacking...and once again he stopped. Rye humped the air, curses and pleas falling from him in equal measure.

"Shhh," Jonas whispered, his mouth over Rye's. Before Rye could kiss—or bite—Jonas returned to his place and worked him with the few final hard strokes it took to have Rye shouting his release and shaking underneath him, spilling over Jonas' hand, his cum spurting onto both of their bodies. Making sure Rye was watching, Jonas dipped a finger in and licked it, head on one side as if unsure about the taste.

Rye opened his mouth, probably to ask a question, and Jonas forced his finger between Rye's lips, smearing his own cum along his tongue. Before Rye could process that, Jonas took a long lick of the cooling spunk and this time stroked his tongue into Rye's mouth, kissing him and sharing his release with him.

"Holy hell!" Rye gasped out when Jonas had finished making Rye's mouth his bitch and pulled back enough for him to speak. "I mean...holy fuck!"

Jonas smiled and gave a nod. Yeah. He'd co-sign that. He loved Rye like this, sweaty, dazed and wearing his mark. Loved that he'd done that to him, that Rye let him. Oh, the things he wanted to do... He ran a hand down Rye's side and turned him enough to stroke down his ass and finger his crease. Rye shivered.

"Should I be afraid of that look in your eyes right now?" he said, his breathing unsteady.

Jonas gave a nod. "Probably. I'm wondering what your ass would look like stuffed with a plug. Oh, not some dainty 'playing at being naughty' plug. A *real* one. The sort referred to as ram-and-cram sized..."

"J-Jonas!" Rye yelped. "You tryin' to get me hard again?"

"Now, why would I do that?" Jonas batted his eyelashes. "When we have to go now?"

"We do?" Rye had evidently forgotten. "We do." He nodded and rolled his eyes as he remembered. "We could always cancel...and stay?"

"Or..." Jonas replied, getting up from the bed. "I could have you wear a plug for the occasion? Or a cock ring?"

He didn't, of course. Not when they'd agreed to spend time with the Intrinsic Value gang, as he sometimes thought of them, and the reason for that being because Aldric had no doubt blabbed about Rye, and Elliot, the store owner, and Drew, his partner, wanted to meet him.

* * * *

"And it had to be at a county fair," Rye groused, taking in the fairground's canvas tents, amusement rides, carnival games and food trailers and carts. He didn't know which was noisier, the mooing and whinnying of livestock from the former or the mechanical music just about covering up the grinding of machinery of the rides. The bells and sirens of the midway games and the yelling and shouting of the people playing them were serious competition too.

"What's wrong with our local county fair?" Jonas asked, all innocence.

"It's a little small?" Rye suggested. Still, it was a good a place as any to help put around the idea that he was merely in town to discharge his duty of guarding the items on loan from the Waco HQ, with plenty of leisure time at his disposal because he wasn't engaged on any clandestine mission, no siree Bob.

Aldric sidled up, dragging Darrell by the hand away from the group of mostly men they were chatting to. Cops, co-workers of Darrell's, Rye thought. Aldric stopped in the middle of greeting him and Jonas and sniffed. "What do I smell?"

"Motor oil? Machinery?" Darrell replied, shaking Rye's hand.

"Nooo…" Aldric tipped his head back to inhale and half-turned to face the row of food tents.

"Oil and grease from deep fryers," Darrell said.

"Hot dogs. Corn dogs. Popcorn. Pretzels. Funnel cakes!"

Aldric looked so comical, inhaling and naming food items that Rye had to grin.

"So, like I said, oil and grease." Darrell shook his head, looking resigned. "Now he won't stop. But wait until we meet up with the others, huh?"

"There's Meredith. And Trent!" Aldric waved wildly. He gaped. "They got their faces painted!"

"And with a couples' theme," Jonas added, with a sly look at Darrell and Aldric.

Aldric took the bait and was still running through ideas with Darrell nixing every one when two other guys joined them.

"Rye, Elliot…" Jonas waved from one to another.

Elliot Douglas was older than Rye had expected, even though he knew the guy owned the business Jonas, Aldric and now Trent worked at, so he'd hardly be some fresh-out-of-school kid. Maybe it was his dress and mannerisms as much as his silvering hair that made him seem middle-aged.

"And Drew Harrington." Elliot's younger and darker-haired partner introduced himself, giving Rye's hand a hard shake. "And yes, the rumors you've heard are true—I'm English. Guilty as charged."

Rye laughed. "That mean I gotta mind my Ps and Qs around you?" he asked, somehow expecting the answer was no.

"The way *he* cusses?" Elliot scoffed. "Of course, you won't understand when he is. That's the good thing about it."

"It's true." Aldric was not so subtly steering the group over to the food trucks as he spoke. "I didn't know what a wanker or a tosser or a bell-end was until I met Drew."

"That…could be taken the wrong way," Drew replied, making Aldric blush and splutter out denials that of course he didn't mean Drew—he'd never say that about him and—

"And I think you need a snack," Darrell said, cutting him off. "Reckon your blood sugar's low. And why do I think it's not gonna be a piece of fruit or a vegetable smoothie?"

"*Chocolate-covered bacon*?" Rye exclaimed, pointing in disbelief at the kiosk selling that item.

"Oh, good idea!" Aldric beamed.

"Oh, man, I'm trying to get Aldric to eat healthier, and here you are sabotaging me!" Darrell exclaimed, smiling.

"Oh, bloody hell." Drew stared at the offering. "It reminds me of being a kid and getting sent to my Scottish relatives, where we'd go to the fish and chip shop and eat chocolate bars deep fried in batter!"

"Iffen y'all like that, look there." Rye pointed at the next stall.

It took Drew two attempts to get the words out. "*F-fried butter*?" he eventually spluttered. "And, oh my God, *fried Coca-Cola*? *How*?"

"A better question would be why," Darrell snarked.

"We can fry anything and put a stick on it in Texas," Meredith explained.

"Playing it safe, eh?" Elliot asked, when all Rye chose was a snow cone.

"Yeah. After I had a slice of scorpion pizza last time I was at a fair…" he replied, then laughed as the group came to a halt and bombarded him with questions left, right and center. He was aware they were feeling him out, getting to know him.

Drew asked questions about the role and remit of Texas Rangers, trying to work out what branch of UK law enforcement they were comparable to, and commenting that they seemed a little like Scotland Yard, where he worked. Elliot was interested in the Ranger artifacts on loan, and Rye's views on pieces from the past in general.

"You must come and visit the store while you're in town," Elliot invited.

Rye guessed he would have tried to ask next how long Rye would be around for, and probably his intentions toward Jonas, but Meredith butted in to describe the restaurant she worked at, in the same block as the antiques store, and that Rye had to come grab lunch there. Oh, and the meatloaf, made with egg and cream, was *so* good… Meredith gave a chef's kiss. "It's to die for."

A shiver rippled down Rye's spine at those words…a second before a loud *bang* rang out behind the party. He whirled around, pushing Jonas to the back of him, and was about to knock him to the ground and cover him when a child let out a huge yell and shook the string in his hand, flapping the limp rubber remnants of what looked to have been a large purple balloon.

The kid next to him squealed too and pointed upward where his balloon, no longer on its string, was drifting up into the air, floating past the spinning rides with their flashing lights. He wailed as he leaped in vain for it.

"That sucks for those kids." Meredith made a sympathetic face at them and their parents. She wasn't the only one concerned—a half dozen people had turned or taken a few steps over to see what the commotion was and were now crowded around the Intrinsic Values people.

"Watch it," Rye said shortly to a couple pressing too close to him and Jonas. They could have knocked Jonas' powdered donut and Rye's shaved ice concoction from their hands. Rye had felt someone jostle against his arm when he'd been distracted — probably this idiot of a guy who sneered and slunk away.

"Aldric, remember when you asked me what a pillock was?" Drew said. He pointed after the male half of the clumsy and uncaring rubbernecking couple. "That's one."

"Oh." Aldric was more interested in his funnel cake.

Rye finished his tutti-frutti flavor snow cone, not really enjoying the last bit, whatever flavor that was. The group walked a little more, and Rye felt his late nights and stress-filled days starting to catch up with him. He didn't exactly have a headache — he didn't suffer from them — but guessed he was tired.

He was glad they left the food stalls behind — their frying onions aroma and fake strawberry cotton candy scents were blocking his nose — even if it was to listen to some folksy music group decked out in denim and kerchiefs, all twanging banjos, ukuleles and teeth-on-edge harmonicas.

When they got to the main part of the fair, the tinny music of the rides blared in his ear and the amplified voices of announcers speaking through microphones echoed around his head. If he'd had any Kleenex on him, he'd have stuffed one in each ear.

"Huh?" he asked Jonas, not catching what he'd said, or why they'd stopped at someplace where flashing lightbulbs danced around a multicolored sign.

"…in here?" Jonas repeated, indicating the group, half of which was already walking in the attraction. "I know. But it might be some fun?"

"House of Fun!" Aldric quipped, nudging them both closer to the garish entrance. "Elliot's got the tickets — come on!"

"I don't think it's a good —" But before Rye finished his sentence, a giant clown mouth swallowed Jonas up, leaving an empty space where he'd been.

Chapter Thirteen

"No!" Rye cried and dove forward...and the House of Fun entrance doors parted and opened again and admitted Rye too. He felt stupid, and more or less fell inside, and was trying to get his bearings when the floor moved in two opposite directions under him, and he grabbed for something—anything—to steady himself.

"Rye?" The English accent clued Rye in that he'd clutched at someone, not something, and that someone was Drew. "Haven't you been in a fun house before?"

"I... Yeah. Of course. Sorry." Rye shoved his hair back from his eyes. "Got a little disorientated. The lights and all?"

It was dark inside and lightbulbs flashed on and off while swinging spotlights cut bright glares through the place and its crowds, making kids squeal when they were lit up.

"I hear you." Drew nodded. He raised his voice over a cackle of recorded laughter that rang around the place. "And look at this section we have to pass through to get to the next room — it's taking me back to my misspent early twenties!"

Rye frowned, trying to understand as he followed Drew, and when he tried to walk along the wall, he got it. The entire wall was a screen, a backdrop for the projection of weirdly colored images, all looking like shapes and blobs to Rye, that morphed one into the next, revolving and dissolving. As if that weren't enough, high-speed strobe lights made everyone appear to be moving in slow motion.

Trent, the young kid who worked the odd day at Elliot's store, was doubled over with laughter, his hands on his knees. "My dad's always telling me I'm so slow I stopped!" he wheezed.

His laughter merged into the shriek of mechanical laughter that filled the place, blasting out again and again.

"Jayden, get off that goddamn clown and stop jumping on its nose!" yelled a young woman, snatching a boy away from a huge clown's face spread out on the floor, its nose a squishy red rubber circle pressure mat.

Rye squeezed his eyes shut tight and shook his head. He even pinched his nose and blew down it, like he did when swimming or diving, to try to clear things. But it didn't work. The effects of the strobes seemed to linger, even though that section of the attraction was left behind them — everyone still moving and speaking slowly.

Until suddenly everything sped up, people squeaking like a record played at the wrong speed and their limbs twitching and flailing about like they'd been Tasered. *What the hell?* This was some average-Joe county fair—why would it have this state-of-the-art equipment?

"Rye, this way!"

Rye grabbed at the words like a lifeline slung to him. He fixed the utterance to a voice then a person, step by slow step. Jonas. Was. Speaking. From a long way off, a great distance. Yeah, he was beckoning back to Rye in a whoosh of movement. "Coming," Rye assured him, unable to tell if he'd yelled or whispered the word. Okay, he must've gotten sick and should get home. Well, to his motel.

"I better catch him up, tell him I'm bailing outta here," Rye said, to whoever was next to him. A small person. Who was the smallest of their group? He tried to think.

"You talking to me, mister? Mister, you okay? *Mom!*" yelled the clown-nose-jumping kid from a minute ago, scrabbling away from Rye to his mother.

Shrugging, Rye set off for Jonas and the others across big round black-and-white swirls—twisting disks he had to cross, one after the other. The guy in front of him was jerked to his knees and stayed there, crawling from one infinity symbol to the next, his curses and complaints sounding like the mooing of cattle against the laughter and jeers of his friends.

Rye didn't have the palms of his hands on the floor—Jesus, it must be nasty with spilled food and drink—but he felt through the soles of his feet the chug of the motor that was powering this ride. So when a gush of steam spilled from a hole in the floor just ahead of him, he nodded in understanding.

He thought he understood how to go through the wooden barrel that was turning and churning in front of him. He just had to walk, crouched over maybe, straight down the middle and let it turn below him and around him and over him. Except he couldn't, because it was full of shuffling, bumping people caught in it yet trying to get up. So he did the next best thing and hoisted himself onto the top of it, to swarm over it on his belly and drop down the other side. He hadn't planned on landing in a heap, though, but his legs were a little unsteady, so he had no choice.

"Rye?" Jonas, his face caught in a flash of orange light, looked at him oddly. He must have waited for him.

"I'm fine," Rye replied to a question that hadn't been asked. He staggered to his feet. "Kindahotinhere, right?" He clawed at his top buttons, wrenching them open. Wait—he wasn't speaking right. He rolled his tongue around the inside of his mouth to check. Both felt swollen, somehow.

"Well, there are balconies up there." Jonas pointed his thumb upward. "If you need fresh air? Or if you need to go, we—"

"Balcony. Air." Rye lurched for the metal handrail of a spiral staircase. A really twisted ladder of a staircase whose rungs weren't level. Maybe that wasn't the best way to ascend. There was an escalator next to it...going down, while people, whooping with laughter, walked up. Rye didn't think he had the coordination for that—he didn't even know if he could stay upright on his own.

"Inner ear thing. Balance thing." He tried to explain why he was clinging to the railing. "Had it before." His fingers hadn't felt numb before though, had they? He frowned at Jonas. "You don't need to think I'm some sorta weakling for it."

"I— What?" Jonas took a step back. "I never said that! Never even thought it. I wouldn't."

Things paused and slowed to a persistent ringing. It took Rye a minute to realize it was him. His pocket. The burner phone in it. He scrabbled for it, and it stopped ringing before he could get it. When he held it, he peered at the message but couldn't read it in this light, so he stumbled toward a lighter patch. And even when he could read the text, it made no sense.

Feeling like an angel?

He held the cell phone closer, and another text appeared.

Because guess who got drugged? Spoiler – you.

It took a half minute for this to sink in, but when it did, Rye broke out in a cold sweat. *Angel, as in dust. As in PCP. No.* He refused to believe it. It wasn't possible…except it was. He tallied his symptoms, his unsteady gait, difficulty speaking, lack of balance, being overheated, numb fingers and yes, toes. "Feelin' like a drunk piece o'shit in general," he muttered.

But beyond that, the way everything seemed *more*. Louder, brighter, slower, faster. Bigger. Smaller. "Heightened sensory perception," he whispered, pulling information from stuff at work. "That's lysergic—"

He jumped when his phone buzzed in his hand.

We dosed you with LSD too.

Outside. He needed to be outside and not in here. "Place is like a goddamn acid trip anyway!" he yelled. He slammed into the wall and shot off it like a pinball ball, then rolled along it until he came to a door with a sign. "E-mer-gen-cy Ex-it." Once he'd spelled the letters into syllables and made them into words he understood, he barreled through it and tumbled out, gulping in the blessed fresh air.

That wouldn't be enough, wouldn't fight the shit he'd been drugged with. The snow cone! And that guy pressing near—classic distraction technique. "Excuse me—" Rye held out a hand to stop a teenage couple who shouldn't have been in this restricted area among the machines and motors but were clearly looking for a place to be alone. "I'll need that." He pointed to the bottle of water the girl held and when she didn't understand, he slid it from her hand, wrenched the top off and chugged it down.

"You got any?" he gasped to the guy, wiping his mouth with the back of his hand.

The guy shook his head, but the girl felt in her shoulder bag and brought out another bottle, this one full and unopened.

"Thank you." Rye felt a little better already as he downed most of the second water.

"Remember it isn't real," the girl said. When Rye stared at her, confused, she shrugged, worldly wise. "Bum trip, right? It can help to chant 'I have what it takes to get through this' as a mantra, you know?"

Rye shook his head, then nodded his thanks before taking a deep breath and heading off. When his phone buzzed another message, he wanted to smash it.

We can get to you at any place. Come meet us at our place.

"How am I supposed to know where that is?" Rye asked his phone.

Hall of Mirrors, came the answer.

Which was *closed for maintenance*, or so the sign said when Rye got there a minute later. The temporary sign, on the main door. So there'd be another door, another way in. He found it. This one was a service door, small and dark, but the space inside was bright with glimmers and glitters of glass.

"A mirror maze," he murmured, swallowing at his reflections and reflections of his reflections. "It's not real," he told the line of Ryes stretching into the distance, growing smaller and thinner and paler as they went. He groped out and saw a dozen arms rise in a line, where the row of mirrors reflected.

"Show yourself!" he yelled, turning away from tiny squat and huge fat Ryes, holding his breath and expecting a hand on his shoulder at any moment. A few paces later the space he was in turned, so he turned with it, to find himself inside a sphere, mirrored all around, but not like the floor-length looking glass in a changing room.

This was all mirrors within mirrors, a kaleidoscope, under flashing lights, showing him everywhere as the moving circular floor beneath his feet spun him in a helpless circle and the mirrors tilted and righted, came forward and receded. He was close and far, everywhere and nowhere and spinning and throwing out an arm only made him hit cold glass.

He wasn't alone. He caught a glimpse of dark hair, once, then again farther down. There could be one man in here with him or a dozen. The revolving floor stopped, leaving him facing a large pane of glass, like the ones in the interview rooms back at HQ…and probably, like that, with people behind it. Well, he could smoke them out. Or rather, shoot them out. If he could remember how to use his gun and get his fingers to cooperate.

"Gabriel Ryland," a voice said. "Currently with Texas Rangers 'F' Company, headquartered at Waco—"

"You asking or telling?" Rye replied. He wanted to listen to the speaker, sure, to glean as much intel on the guy's background, age, ethnicity, social status or whatever as he could. But he also wanted to rile up whoever had lured him here. Oh, and fucking drugged him.

"Formerly a Texas Highway Patrol Trooper trained at the Department of Public Safety headquarters in Austin—"

"You writin' my résumé for me?" Rye interrupted. "And I take it I ain't up before some HR panel here, so why not show yourselves?" He finished the last sip of water and cast the bottle aside. "Oh and why drug me, you fuckin' cowards?"

"Like we said, to show you we can get to you anywhere," the voice answered. "And it wasn't anywhere near OD levels…this time."

Hispanic. Rye would stake his life on it…and hoped he didn't have to. "Camargo, right? So, what, I'm getting to you and you brought me here to kill me?"

The voice laughed and said something in Spanish before switching back to English. "If we wanted to kill you, you'd already be dead, *cabrón*. No. We brought you here to bribe you."

Rye had expected that. "Oh yeah? How much?" The amount of money the voice mentioned had him staggering. "That's monthly, of course," he quipped, thinking it must be a one-off payment.

"Of course." The voice was getting impatient.

"I got three words in reply." Rye raked his gaze along the glass. "Go to hell."

A sigh reached his ears. "Last chance," a different voice said, and Rye braced himself...only to have a higher figure thrown at him.

"How about, I'm gonna see you burn?" Rye said in answer.

"We got no problem taking you out," the second voice told him.

"Do that and every scrap of evidence I have gets released to every law enforcement agency, police department and media outlet from here to Washington," Rye lied.

"Fine. Next stage."

Rye had no chance for a smart answer or a question—lights blinded him and sirens deafened him, forcing him almost to his knees. A clang behind him was a door opening and he staggered to it—and through it. Someone reached out a hand to him and Rye went to punch—

"Rye, it's me!" Jonas caught him and dragged him to a dark corner in the shadow of some machinery. "What happened? Where did you go?"

"They got to me. Got a message to me, I mean." Still groggy, Rye didn't want to admit he'd been drugged. "On my phone."

But when he took it out to show Jonas, none of the messages from the cartel remained. "They must have some program, some tech that erases them after a few minutes." He cursed.

"This...this..." Jonas shook his head, his lips compressed. "Is serious. Rye, you might not be happy about this, but I told Darrell. And I'm glad I did"—he raised his voice over Rye's attempt at protest— "because when I saw something was going on just now, I told the others you got food poisoning and Darrell stayed to help me. He's here."

Right here, Rye discovered when Darrell came over from where he'd been lurking, checking carefully all around first. Jonas filled him in. If the SAPD sergeant thought Rye had acted rashly, he kept it to himself.

"Okay, so we can add attempted bribery of a LEO to the list." Darrell straightened his shoulders. "This has gone too far. You know that, right?" He spoke to both of them. "We got no other recourse but to hand this upward. So you are both gonna come to the station when I'm on shift a little later. I'll set things up, and we'll get everything documented, written, audio and video. Then take it from there."

* * * *

Rye wouldn't have agreed if he wasn't still groggy. Back at Jonas', he took the longest shower on record and drank another gallon of water while he was in there, trying to get the shit out of his system and sober up. Thank fuck those bastards had only slipped him a mild dose. That girl who'd helped him probably took a lot more recreational drugs, and routinely.

Even after he shut the water off, he stayed in there, letting the steam and Jonas' eucalyptus-scented shower tablets—something Rye had never even heard of— bring him back to his right mind. Was this the best plan? The lack of evidence, of proof, of—

"*Rye!*"

"I'm coming out," he assured Jonas, who was barging in, sounding half hysterical. "I was just tired, thought the steam…" He took in Jonas' stricken face and the cell phone in his hand. "What? What, Jonas?"

Jonas swallowed. "It's Darrell…"

Chapter Fourteen

"And you still don't know any more?" Rye asked again, sparing Jonas a look then returning his attention to the road. He swerved to switch lanes.

Jonas, eyes on his phone, willing more information to come through it, shook his head. "Aldric hasn't said anything else after that one text and isn't replying at all." He reread the stark, horrifying message saying that Darrell had been found severely injured near his car and taken to hospital. Reading it yet again didn't make it any more understandable.

"So it was a crash, a road traffic accident, and he was thrown from the vehicle?" he wondered out loud. Again.

Rye pointed at the radio. "Nothing on any channel about a major crash."

"Why major?" Jonas asked.

"To fit your scenario? We'd be talking high-speed, heavy impact. Streets would be closed." Rye shook his head. "Try again?"

Jonas pressed Call again. "Nothing. I think his phone must be off now."

"In the hospital? I'd say so," Rye replied.

Jonas lifted his gaze from his cell. "This isn't the way to the Regional."

"It's the way we're going," Rye answered.

Oh of course. They were taking a roundabout route, looping back on themselves and using smaller secondary roads. It was necessary...wasn't it? Jonas wasn't sure about anything anymore. But he did know that it added time to their journey.

"Maybe...it's not...what we're thinking," he tried to say. That this, whatever it was, was a senseless accident, terrifying and awful for everyone concerned...and nothing to do with them. His words, what he was trying to do with them, felt so cowardly, and he felt ashamed for uttering them. For thinking them. With a muttered "Sorry," he fell silent.

Rye squeezed his leg and neither he nor Jonas spoke for the rest of the way.

"Thank God!" Jonas exclaimed as Rye parked, and they hurried from the car into the bright antiseptic of the hospital.

"Hey—" The security guard trying to slow their run melted back when Rye flashed his ID.

"Darrell Williams," Jonas panted. "He was brought in—maybe to ER?"

Surgical Unit, they learned, after the guard took them to a receptionist behind a plexi-glass barricade, who took an age finding information on her computer.

"Surgery?" Jonas gasped the word, looking at Rye. "But why? What happened?"

"I'm not permitted to disclose that information." The woman finally looked up, and what she saw in their faces seemed to soften her a little. "Please try to understand."

"We..." Jonas gave up on speech and just nodded. "May we...I don't know...wait?"

"Surely." The receptionist used a walkie-talkie to summon an orderly. "Surgical Ward," she murmured to the uniformed man, then jerked her head at Rye. "LEO."

Jonas remembered Aldric telling him and Elliot, after his first date with Darrell, that Darrell got special treatment because he was a law enforcement officer. *"He even gets to cut in line!"* he'd said, amazed. *"Oh, he doesn't cut in – the other people tell him to go ahead, before them! And I think the taco truck man gave him a bigger serving!"*

Well, if Rye being a Ranger got them to see Darrell, Jonas would be happy about it too.

"Hate hospitals," Rye muttered as they hurried down long, maze-like corridors and crossed hallways whose shiny tile flooring reflected the overhead fluorescent lighting, following signs. "Hate the damn smell, even."

Jonas nodded. He hated the sounds, the electrical buzz of the strip lighting, the burbles over the intercoms, the squeal and clang of carts and wheelchairs. Everything seemed to echo and bounce back, making the place feel claustrophobic.

The orderly stopped outside a door and when he opened it, everyone inside sprang to their feet, subsiding when Jonas and Rye walked in. Everyone except Aldric, who looked like he'd been pacing to and fro from the door to the water cooler on the opposite wall. Not that there was a lot of floor to pace.

"Aldric!" Jonas rushed to him. He wasn't demonstrative by nature but hugged his co-worker. His friend. "What happened?"

Aldric shook his head, and Elliot steered him into a seat. "I don't know!" he wailed. "Someone from the station called me and told me what I told you. He got into work but left without saying where he was going. They'd been trying to get him on his cell and were about to call home—me—when someone reported in that a man was lying near his car." He paused and accepted a plastic cup of water from Elliot.

"And when the license plate was read, it was Darrell's?" Rye finished the story for him.

"And the injuries are so severe he needed immediate emergency surgery." Aldric's hand shook so much he slopped some of the water over the side of the cup.

Jonas took it from him and placed it on the table among the old magazines.

"He's in a good place." Elliot waved a hand to indicate the hospital, not this shabby waiting room. "This hospital has a good reputation."

The door opened again, and this time Jonas was one of those springing up, not the cause of it. And once again, they all sank down as an elderly woman, the handkerchief she held in one hand to dab at her eyes covering most of her face, stumbled in.

"Ma, careful!" a middle-aged woman following her said. "Sit down before you fall down! Look, Dad's tough. You know that. He'll make it. And he wouldn't want you to be like this, would he?" She led her mother to the seats at the other end of the room, glaring at everyone already there as if they were intruding.

Rye took the box of Kleenex from the ledge that held the water cooler and placed it on the far edge of the table, near the two women. "Get you some water, ladies?" he offered, getting tight head shakes in reply.

It hadn't occurred to Jonas that the waiting room was a general one, but of course it was, and for all Elliot's words about how top tier this place was, the room, with its dog-eared magazines on the table and its generic artworks on the walls, was depressing.

The door didn't burst open this time because the women had left it open, so the man filling the doorway then barreling in made Jonas jump.

"Darrell?" the guy asked, looking from one to another of their small group.

Jonas knew him. His uniform gave away his job and his rusty-red hair made him memorable. Officer O'Hara was Darrell's former partner, before Darrell had made sergeant.

"Still in surgery," Aldric replied. "Sean, what do you know?"

"Hi." The female officer with Sean gave them all a half-wave, a flutter of her fingers. "We don't know much—"

"Officer Laurie Strauss. My new partner," Sean interrupted. "Well, I say new. It's been…ooh, how long now?"

"Please!" Aldric begged.

Sean glanced around and pulled up a plastic chair to huddle close to the group, then stopped, looking at Rye. Aldric had his hand over his mouth as the two introduced themselves. "It seems he stopped and got out of his car," Sean began. "Maybe he was responding to a suspicious vehicle or person."

Or it stopped him. Jonas bet Rye was thinking the same.

"And he could have disturbed someone or someones. Maybe they were actively involved in criminal activity or had an active warrant out, and so, on seeing a patrol officer, thought..." Laurie was too kind to finish. "But word is there was a physical altercation."

"Shots fired?" Rye demanded.

Aldric grabbed Elliot's hand.

"No reports of gunfire, so the belief is no weapon discharged," Sean answered.

"Oh, thank God." Aldric heaved out a long breath, some of his color returning.

"No damage to his vehicle either." Sean shrugged.

"Let's be grateful he was taken to hospital so quickly," Elliot said.

Footsteps bustled up outside in the corridor, too brisk and competent to be anything other than a medical professional, and Aldric was on his feet even before a white-uniformed nurse appeared in the doorway.

"Mrs. Rensin?" she asked, directing her attention at the elderly woman, her smile reassuring. "Your husband is out of surgery now and we're happy to say all went well. If you'd like to come with me...?"

The woman's attempts at speech were muffled in her tissue, and her daughter, bombarding the nurse with questions when her mother couldn't, supported her from the room.

"Should we have asked her for any news?" Jonas asked Rye in a mutter, indicating the nurse who'd just left.

"Don't guess so," Rye whispered back. "She'd have said. Or someone would, if there was anything to tell us. We—"

He broke off as footsteps marched down the corridor. There was no other way to describe the speed and purpose of the beats that rang out. A second later, a man filled the doorway, and Jonas' mouth fell open at his resemblance to Darrell. He was an older, taller, broader version, in a different uniform, with similar-enough hair and eyes to proclaim a relationship between himself and Darrell.

He simply stood, framed by the doorway, raking everyone present with his gaze, as if taking their measure, or feeling out the room. "Darrell Williams?" he demanded, his voice a deep command, yet tight.

Elliot was the first to reply, on his feet and shaking his head. "He's— Well, we don't know."

He received a short, sharp nod in reply before the man turned with military precision and marched out. "Darrell Williams!" he called. Not shouted or yelled— Jonas would guess he didn't need to. He'd seen professors like that in his time teaching, ones who barely had to raise their voice to exert their authority. "Where is my *son*?"

His voice stretched tighter to almost break as he said the latter part, and the corridor went into a bustle and flurry in response. "*Chief*?" Jonas heard someone say. Not that he needed that extra clue to tell him who the man was.

"Have you met Major Williams before?" he asked Aldric, who shook his head.

"I've always asked Darrell to extend invitations to his father and both brothers for any celebration or event we hold," Elliot said.

He didn't need to say none were accepted. Jonas had met Darrell's younger brother and his fiancée at a five-a-side soccer game—Darrell and Jonas played on a team—but not the others.

"Let me guess. All military?" Rye asked.

"San Antonio *is* the Military City," Sean said, bristling a little. Laurie's hand on his arm calmed him. "Since Darrell…" He waved a finger at Aldric, then at Elliot and Jonas, perhaps to include them or make his meaning clear, then stopped, looking appalled. "No, I don't mean… *Jesus*." He scrubbed his hand over his face. "I'm trying to say that there's only his younger brother, Ryan, and Leah, who, well…"

"That he gets on with," Laurie suggested, a blander version of the Williams' family dynamics.

"Yeah," Sean agreed. "Good way to put it." He pulled her to him.

Jonas was fairly sure the SAPD officer was engaged…to a different woman, but what did Jonas know about heterosexual relationships? There was the concept of the work spouse, wasn't there? Things fell into a lull and Jonas into a doze, jerking in reaction occasionally to raised voices along the corridor, meaning he was groggy when Rye shook him awake.

"C'mon, hun. He said we can go see…"

The guy Rye jerked his head toward wasn't in uniform, but his strong build in his crisp slacks and rolled-sleeve button-up shirt gave him the look of the off-duty military personnel Jonas saw about the city. But this wasn't Ryan? Still half-asleep, Jonas followed their group to the Critical Care Unit and a small private room that the glass door showed to be sterile white, dotted with softly beeping equipment and machines and holding a single bed.

"Darrell!" Aldric cried, tears streaming down his face, and rushed in...to be stopped by the tall broad man at the door.

"No," Darrell's father said, his face more heavily lined than it had been. He also looked less pristine than he had before. The man who'd escorted them, similar-enough-looking that he had to be the elder Williams brother, gave a brief pat to his father's shoulder then dropped his hand.

"But—" Aldric started. "We—"

"Don't care." Major Williams crossed his arms. "No admittance without being gowned and gloved up. Risk of infection and I'm taking no risks. Understood?"

Jonas wasn't sure he did, especially when the major continued, "I had them go get extra sets now. They're on their way." He gave a crisp nod.

"Then I can go in?" Aldric sounded very young as he almost begged.

"We can, yes." Major Williams swallowed.

"What happened, sir?" Sean asked.

"Officer O'Hara." Darrell's father acknowledged him but didn't answer.

"He was beaten." Ryan, the younger son, stepped forward to speak. "Like, set upon, by more than one person. Couple of broken bones, some internal bruising...they thought possible organ damage." He turned his head away.

"If I discover who did this..." Major Williams didn't need to complete his promise.

"And deep slashes down his chest, through skin and muscle, almost to the organs," the other brother said. "That's the real fucking damage. Pardon me, ma'am." He nodded to Laurie. "Slashes like claws." He dragged his nails down his chest to illustrate.

Oh no. The world started to close in around the edges for Jonas and he struggled for air. He looked at Rye and Rye looked back.

"*Claws?*" Sean asked. "Like, the weapon, the tiger claw, Travis? Or lion's paw? The *bagha*? That's a gang thing. I mean, *serious* gangs."

"Organized crime gangs?" the major asked, his voice dagger-sharp.

"I don't know—" Sean broke off to allow a nurse pushing a small trolley to get into the room. "I don't know what Darrell was working on but…could be."

"Then this might have repercussions. My son's room will need a round-the-clock guard," his father demanded.

"Jesus God Almighty. That might take a while to put through," Sean started to reply, looking at Laurie.

"Then I'll do it, boy." The major stood straight. "His family will have his back. We need more men, I'll get ones I trust from Lackland AFB."

"And me from the Special Operations Aviation Regiment," Travis promised.

"Rest assured anyone who's not supposed to get close to him won't." Major Williams sucked in a breath. "I might not agree with a lot of what Darrell chooses to do…" He narrowed his eyes at Aldric.

"It's not a choice. I explained earlier," Ryan butted in.

"Are you contradicting me?" his father demanded.

"Yes. Sir." Ryan gave a nod.

Had that been what the raised voices had been about earlier, the youngest son standing up to their father? Something had happened, and sadly, stupidly, it often took a tragedy or a near-tragedy to make people appreciate what they had.

The major glared at Ryan, who refused to be cowed. His father was the one to drop his gaze. He exhaled. "Fine. I don't understand a lot of what my son does, but he's a good, courageous police officer who's served the public and proved his worth over and over, and, more importantly, he's my *son*. Always had been, always will be. That's all there is to it."

He held out his hand to Aldric, who stared at it, then, at a nudge from Elliot, slowly shook it. The nurse opened the door from inside and held out two sealed packs of gowns, and the major and Aldric took one each.

All Jonas could do was peer over at the lone figure in the small bed, the horror of the attack and the situation a lead weight in his heart.

Chapter Fifteen

The shadows stretching across the ground from each wall of each building lengthened and wavered. It wasn't just the walls—every curve of whatever fabric the small huts were made from, every angle to them seemed to grow its own night-black twin that made the entire scene darker by the second. Rye knew what was coming before it happened, but even struggling, trying to reach out to stop it made no difference.

The doors to the hut were flung open and men rushed out, all armed, and all firing, the bangs of the shots loud and the flares of white magnesium and silver bullets piercing the pitch-black of the night.

"No!" Rye shouted…as did Chip, his hands raised in surrender and to cover his head and face, as if that would protect him, make him bulletproof. And Rye couldn't help, couldn't run to his partner's assistance—his feet were stuck to the tar-like substance he stood in, something that was soft enough for him to be sinking into it. Within a second, he'd sunk to his knees, and no amount of flailing his arms made any difference.

The group of armed men, black-clad from head to foot so they blended into the night, turned to him. The hoods over their faces meant he couldn't make out even one of their features, couldn't identify them if he saw them on the street.

They pointed, but not their weapons — their fingers, and laughed, rocking and swaying, the cackles mechanical, as were they, stupid rolling laughing dolls, like in the fun house. Maybe it was the boiling-hot rage consuming Rye at the men who'd murdered his partner in front of him finding it funny that helped Rye to move.

Whatever it was that gave him the strength or agility to free himself from the quicksand-like trap, he was out and rushing to the nearest man, his fist raised...to collide with glass. The man wasn't real. Only a reflection. Snarling, Rye turned to the next, and punched, only to hit his hand on another mirror. The third, Rye swung both arms up over his head and brought them down in a punishing hammer blow, and this shattered the glass. He pushed through, the shards tearing his clothes and skin — to find nothing.

He was howling in rage and crying tears of frustration when he woke, sweat-soaked and tangled in the sheets of his motel room bed. He woke alone — Jonas wasn't there. He had been, yesterday, when they'd driven back from the hospital. He'd even stayed a while, both of them lying side by side on this bed, holding each other, unable to sleep of course.

"The elephant in the room got bigger," Rye had said at last, acknowledging the horror that had happened.

Jonas had nodded. He checked his watch. "I have to go. What...what's the next step?"

Rye was fucked if he knew. "I'll figure it out," he'd promised. And he hadn't gone into work yesterday, doing just that instead, documenting everything and making lists of law enforcement officers he could trust—he thought. Guys he knew from training, or in other branches. He even had a vague contact in the FBI. He—

The knocking at the door had him rolling from the bed and crouching at its other side, his gun in his hand.

"Rye?" the woman called. "Ranger Gabriel Ryland, you in there?"

"*Lina?*" Startled at the idea of Chip Daniels' widow *here*, Rye was on his feet, straightening up the bed with one hand and shoving his gun down the back of his sweatpants with the other. He tried to pull the wrinkles from his pants and tee, and make his hair look less like bedhead as he crossed to the door. "It is you!" he exclaimed, opening the door a crack and trying to disguise the fact he was peering around the forecourt and parking area.

"Can I come in?" Lina asked and took a step forward without waiting for an answer.

Well, they'd always been casual, the Daniels' house open to Rye and his to them. Standing on ceremony now would be weird, even in this motel room. At least it wasn't messy—he'd locked all his notes in the safe. But it was shabby and worn. Lina prettied it up, though.

"It's good to see you," Rye said, meaning it. She looked a lot better than when he'd last seen her. She still wore dark clothes, but had some color to her face, and her hair was styled, not covered by a mantilla. "Can't say I was expecting you any, though?"

"I'm sorry." Lina huddled in on herself.

"No, for God's sake!" Rye helped her off with her coat and hung it on the back of the door. He pulled out the chair at the desk, but she didn't sit.

"I just had to get away for a while." Lina perched on the edge of the desk. "From the family. I know that sounds awful and ungrateful…"

"No. I think I get it." She had two sisters and was close to her parents, especially her mom. Chip had often complained that Dulce, as his mother-in-law insisted he call her, played too active a role in Lina's, and so his, life, dictating everything from their meals to the furnishings they chose for their house.

Rye would bet Dulce had moved in to take care of Lina for a while. "People are doing all they can, what they think is best, but you needed some time to yourself. Some breathing room."

"I guess. I knew you'd understand." She smiled her thanks. "Just a few hours, you know? See somewhere different… I kind of just got in the car and drove. I only understood I was heading for Hamilton Pool when I got there."

"The waterfall? In the cliffs and grottoes?" Rye had been hiking in the park there and had swum in the limestone rockpool but couldn't believe Lina would want to.

Lina's smile turned sad. "Chip and I used to go there when we were dating. Or courting, as his father called it." She shared a grin with Rye at one of Declan Daniels' words. "But it was closed, and now you need a reservation to go in there! So instead of turning around and heading home, I carried on and came here. Guess I've missed seeing you about."

She leaned back and her skirt fell open at the slit up its side. "So, how's it all going? You're assigned to a traveling exhibition of historical Ranger stuff, right? Old records and bygones? I couldn't really understand, but I guess it's until they pair you up with a new partner?"

"I guess." That was the official story.

"Won't be anyone like Chip, though." Lina's face crumpled a little.

"That's for sure." And probably for more reasons than Lina knew.

"Is it fun? The display and the little history museum here, I mean." Lina pushed herself off from the edge of the desk. "I'd like to see it. Maybe you could show it to me? Or even show me around town? The center is real pretty — at least in pictures — with that little river and all the places along its banks. It looks like Europe! Not that I ever went..." She moved, as if looking around the nondescript room, and it brought her closer to him.

"I haven't gotten out and about much." Rye spoke slowly, trying to understand Lina's mood...or even her intentions. "But yeah, San Antonio is nice."

"So you can understand why Chip liked it? Least, he seemed to."

Rye didn't know what to say to that, or the new expression on Lina's face. "I'm so sorry about what happened, Lina," he said. "If I could go back to that night—"

"Sometimes it's not about going back." Lina interrupted him. "Sometimes it's about going forward. Moving on, you know?" She took another step and closed the gap between them.

"Lina?" She was suddenly much too close. Rye went to take a step back at the same time as Lina brought up her hand to cup his cheek. "What are y'all doing?" he demanded, raising his hand to cover hers and drop it down. "Y'all know I'm gay and—"

"And not bi? I thought...thought you might find me attractive." Lina tried to wrap her fingers around his.

What the hell? The clutch of her fingers felt as off as that catch to her voice. "No." Rye gave a shake of his head and set her hand free. "*No*, Lina. I mean yeah, you're pretty, and I understand you're hurting, missing Chip, and need some comfort, but..." He wondered if he should offer her a hug—they'd embraced like that a hundred times, over the years—but didn't want any misunderstanding. "Let me get y'all a coffee." The room had a coffeemaker, thank God, and he needed a cup.

"I'm sorry. Rye—please." Lina bit her lip. "Let's just talk, huh?" She sounded almost jolly now, and her lightning switches of mood were confusing the hell out of him. "So you haven't been along the Riverwalk? What have you seen here in town? Been to any bars?"

"Oh, I did go to a county fair." He forced his tone to be as light as hers. "Nice enough but not a patch on the Heart O' Texas Fair and Rodeo."

"So, no bars or clubs?" Lina asked again and the hairs on the back of Rye's neck stood up.

He wasn't a good gambler like Jonas, with his uncanny ability to see people's tells, but he was a law enforcement officer, trained to read people...even if he didn't like what he was seeing. "Say, how d'ya know I was here at this motel?" he asked, his tone so casual he sounded country bumpkin. "I don't recall tellin' y'all?"

"Didn't you? Well, you didn't have to. The HQ always puts its Rangers up here, when they come to SA."

"Like Chip," Rye said, as if it were a fact, and Lina nodded.

Except...Chip hadn't stayed here. If he had been in SA on Ranger business, it would be a fucking coincidence if he'd come here, because Rye had chosen the place himself, from ones he researched that were within his per diem budget. *Oh, Jesus.* "I did go to a bar, yeah, to answer your question," he said, stepping closer to Lina as he spoke. "Two actually, although neither were what you'd call a normal drinking place."

"Oh?" she replied.

"Yeah. One was that cards club you mentioned and the other was a pool hall." Right on top of her now, he raised his voice. "You getting all this? Need me to speak up more? Oh, and where's the wire?"

"The—?" Lina's words ended in a shriek as Rye ripped open her blouse to expose the black square of the mic she wore.

Shit. Disgust warred with fear in him. He felt ice-cold but fanned the ember of hope that still burned in him, because he wanted so hard to believe that even this was innocent, that she was maybe assisting in some official inquiry, checking into his story of the night Chip was killed. It was possible, wasn't it? He tried to think who would know which motel he'd chosen. "Who sent you? Lieutenant LeGrande?"

Lina didn't react to the name, just folded her ripped blouse around her chest, her expression somewhere between defiant and scared. "You always think you have to be the one who handles everything, don't you?" she spat at him as she stalked to the door.

She grabbed her coat and flung the door open…just as Jonas came walking up. Or more properly, 'Joe' because Jonas had a baseball cap pulled down low and was wearing the sort of clothes he wouldn't for the university.

"Lina…" Rye wanted to make a last attempt to talk. To listen. To learn. To avenge. To *something*.

"Don't." She pulled her coat on, her ruined blouse falling open. "Don't speak to me. Don't contact me. Nothing. You hear, Rye?" She almost tripped in her haste to get to her car and get away.

Jonas watched, as Rye did, and only when the car had gone did he sidle in, his face one huge question. Rye suddenly realized how things could seem.

"It's not what it looks like," he started.

"It's not an attractive woman running out of your motel room, her with her clothes ripped, and you not really wearing any?" Jonas inquired.

"She's not just a woman. She's Lina Daniels. Chip's wife. Widow." Rye raked his hands through his hair. "And she was here to pump me for information. She's in on it, Jonas!"

"She's— And you let her walk out?" Jonas rounded on him—the question replaced by suspicion.

"Not because there's anything between us!" Rye protested. "We're friends—well, I thought we were, but…"

The sight of Jonas there, confusion in his beautiful brown eyes, his pink lips open as if he were about to speak made all the helpless longing in Rye boil over. He grabbed Jonas, cupping his butt to bring him close, and moaned at how Jonas' ass fit his hands perfectly. He lowered his head and brushed his mouth over Jonas'. He didn't dive right in, though he burned to, just let his body talk for him.

He moved a hand up to Jonas' nape, keeping the touch of lips to his. He loved the feel of Jonas' mouth, his soft, warm lips, the whisper of his breath. He firmed the hand he still had on Jonas' ass and pressed his mouth to his. He'd thought about tasting Jonas' lips, feathering his tongue over that sweet bottom lip, that sharper top one, but Jonas took the lead, slipping his tongue inside Rye's mouth and dominating him effortlessly.

Rye stumbled back, hitting the closed door. He was lost in Jonas' taste, in his heat and dominance. The kiss lengthened and deepened, their mutual need and arousal tangible between them. Rye felt the rigid heat of Jonas' cock through Jonas' jeans and his sweatpants, and his own dick responded, leaking pre-cum. Jonas sucked on Rye's tongue, leaving him gasping, then trailed wet kisses down Rye's jaw to his neck. Whenever he nipped a sweet spot, Rye thrust.

"Jonas," he whispered, his breath catching. "I want you. Fuck, I want you so bad. I've never wanted anyone the way I want you."

The low growl Jonas made in response brought every nerve ending along Rye's spine alive. He had to move, rocking and rubbing against Jonas, seeking that perfect friction. They could rut here, or on the bed.

Casting a look at the bed, Rye's glance caught on the desk. Lina had been there. Suddenly suspicious, he pulled free from Jonas, as difficult as that was, and crossed the few steps to the plain wooden table, ubiquitous to any cheap hotel or motel room.

"What—?"

Rye's finger to his lips, visible when he turned back to Jonas, cut off Jonas' question. There was nothing new on the desk, but underneath... His patting fingers found a small black square stuck on. Those weren't common to all motels. Cheap motels had bugs, but this—

"*She planted a mic,*" Rye mouthed, pointing at it. He tried to think if he'd just used Jonas' name, or if Jonas had spoken, revealing information.

Oh God, what if she left a fuckin' camera too?

Chapter Sixteen

"We have to get out of here," Rye mouthed, and Jonas nodded. They did. The plural pronoun struck Jonas…in its rightness.

How had this become his life? Or how had his life become this? Jonas was a historian, not a philosopher, so didn't know how he should frame the question. What he did know was that he missed Gabriel Ryland so much when he was apart from him that he suspected what he felt was love. He looked at him now, taking in Rye's dark-blond hair and blue eyes, his corded-muscled body now encased in tight jeans, boots and hat as Rye threw on clothes. The pull Jonas felt went beyond the physical, however.

He appreciated that Rye lived by a moral code and was determined to do the right thing and that he was floundering at the turn events had taken. Jonas knew how that felt. What Rye was going through reinforced the fact that he and Jonas were kindred spirits, just as their kinks lined up and the big strong Ranger needed to hand over control as much as Jonas was fulfilled by exercising it.

Jonas watched Rye fold and pack the few possessions he had here in San Antonio into his duffel, reflecting on how each new thing he discovered or learned about Rye added to his attraction. His interest in cooking yet weakness for sweet things. His love of country rock, that he played while driving or cooking, even if it made Jonas roll his eyes. His pride in his job, his service, and how he understood Jonas felt the same about his, even though Jonas' calling was of a different nature, and a career he'd felt increasingly unsure about lately, especially since meeting Rye.

Rye's dedication to duty shone like a beacon. That he understood something had happened to derail Jonas' career trajectory and felt sympathy for him over it without pressing for details Jonas wasn't ready to share… Jonas could love him for that alone.

He could have laughed because he'd come here today wanting to share that episode with Rye. He'd wanted to pour out the shock and pain of the false accusation, one originating in the way Jonas had stuck to his core beliefs, his refusal to bend, to pretend. Rye would understand that and the way people Jonas had considered friends couldn't quite meet his eyes and weren't lining up to be character witnesses in his defense, refuting the charges based on their knowledge of him.

Instead, none of his colleagues had wanted to rock the boat or make waves—Jonas had lost count of the nautical metaphors dealt out like a weak hand of cards in a low-stakes poker game. He was better at similes than his 'friends' were at metaphors. *Just go quietly*, he'd been urged, in tones varying from pleas to orders. *The college can't afford a scandal and neither can you. Much easier to start over somewhere else.*

"Ready," Rye said quietly, close to Jonas' ear. He hefted his bag.

Jonas bit his lip. He still wallowed in self-pity, whereas Rye was practically on the run, probably looking for an even more rundown motel, in a worse area than this one. No. Jonas wanted him. To be with him. "The cartel know you're here, and I bet they know the museum," he whispered. Rye nodded. "They don't know my place…"

Rye grinned, despite all that was going on. "You asking me to move in with you?" His grin soon faded. "Jonas, I can't put you in danger like that. In fact, the responsible thing to say would be that we should stop seeing each other. But I can't. I'm in too deep with you." He dropped his duffel and pulled Jonas in tight. No one had ever hugged him like Rye did, folding him into his arms, so he could be warmed by his heat, inhale his scent.

He wanted to stay there all day but eased back. "So what's the plan?"

"Get somewhere so I can call things in on a conference call to all three of my superior officers who I have to report this to. This is a Rangers matter."

The way he said it, Jonas saw there was little use trying to persuade him to deliver this to a different law enforcement body. Elliot had a contact in the FBI, as unlikely as that sounded, but… Jonas considered their options. "Follow me to campus? You can set up in the department office, use the computer and phone?"

As he said the last word, his cell rang, and he pulled it from his pocket. Number unknown. "Hello?" he answered, only for the connection to drop. Or be dropped. Again. How many times had that happened, recently? Well, they had more pressing issues to deal with than the shortcomings of Jonas' cell phone network.

He got another dropped call ten minutes later, when he was driving ahead of Rye's pickup truck, with a careful two or three cars between them, leading the way to campus. When he got the third, Jonas had had enough. "Listen to me, you little cretin. Yes, *cretin*, if you can't work a cell phone in this day and age. Or if you can and choose not to, you're a coward. So which is it?"

He strained to hear and thought he could catch the sound of breathing, as if the caller had gasped then bitten the sound off. Good. "Whichever it is, come face me like a man." He cut the connection and focused on the road.

A few minutes later, he wished he hadn't issued the challenge. *No, I'm being stupid. Paranoid...but that doesn't mean that Dodge Challenger isn't following me.* Jonas slowed, to the point that drivers behind him sounded their irritation and opinion of his driving and his Jetta, but the SUV didn't overtake.

"Rye?" Jonas kept his voice as steady as he could when he called him. "Tell me I'm being fanciful, that a challenge didn't manifest a Challenger?"

"I dunno what that means, Prof, but I see a pursuit vehicle, yep."

Jonas appreciated Rye aiming for casual. Breezy, even. "And?"

"And you carry on drivin', sugar."

Jonas did, fear flickering stronger through him every time he glimpsed the black SUV. He felt in the glove compartment for his loaned Glock, thinking how unreal this was. He was a mild-mannered history professor…okay, fine, a borderline compulsive gambler thrill seeker. Well, he'd found 'em. "Can I stay on the line?" he begged Rye, not wanting to hang up and be alone. He did as Rye had said and continued heading for the campus. "That vehicle's aptly named, huh?"

"That heap o' junk?" Rye scoffed. "See that church coming up there?"

"It's the university church. Sorry, you didn't need to know that. I didn't need to say that. I don't even know why it's called that or what it means." Jonas slammed his lips together to stop talking.

Rye laughed. "You're so goddamn cute when you babble. Good thing I ain't one o'your students, sittin' in a lecture hall listenin' to you. I'd have a hard-on the size of Houston."

"I don't babble in lectures!" Jonas replied indignantly but liked that he turned Rye on. Thinking about Rye aroused had Jonas shifting in his seat. "What about the church, Field Ranger Ryland?"

"Turn into the parking then pull around the side. The back if you can."

Jonas had to do so sharply — the church was right there. He peeled around to the side as far as he could go then braked in a heap. He snatched at the phone, but Rye must have disconnected the call. *Great. Now what? Gun,* he answered himself. Before he got it out, the Challenger was behind him, squealing to a halt. The driver's-side door flew open before the engine stopped and, peering in the rear-view mirror showed booted feet swinging themselves to the ground. Jonas' entire body shook with the fear coursing through it that was a response to the torrent of thoughts flooding his mind. *Is this it, how things end?*

The man stepped fully out and— "What?" Jonas cried. It was someone Jonas had never expected to see again. "What?" Jonas repeated and swung out of his car to check. "*Braydon?*"

"Professor Abrams." Braydon smirked down at him. He was still tall and big, but a lot of the muscle had gone to fat. He looked as arrogant and entitled as ever, but desperation lurked in his eyes. He looked crazed around the edges. The smirk turning into a sneer, he went to speak, but Rye's truck pulling up hard and fast behind him had him jumping out of the way and cursing.

Rye was on the ground in a heartbeat. "Step away from him," he ordered Braydon.

"You got a bodyguard?" Braydon wiped the back of his hand across his mouth. "Yeah, you need one for wrecking lives!"

That Rye might be wondering if Braydon was an ex made Jonas feel ill. "Braydon was a student of mine when I taught in Dallas."

"Was." Braydon mimicked Jonas in a sickly voice. "Until you fucking got me kicked out!"

"You got yourself kicked out," Jonas snapped. "For not doing the work. You knew you needed to keep your grades up to keep your place." Jonas looked at Rye to see if he was following.

"Lemme guess. Sports, free ride?" Rye said. "And you took all the easy courses to meet the terms of your scholarship."

They'd called those electives names like "rocks for jocks" or "animal planet" when Jonas was studying in college, but by the time he was teaching in one, athletes called them "guts" courses—ones with light workloads, easy grading or hopefully both.

"And couldn't even hack those?" Rye continued.

"There was supposed to be an easy track for sports stars!" Braydon howled. "Like, just show up at a weekly one-hour lecture and get given a multiple-choice quiz at the end of the semester! But no. Not with the high and mighty Professor Abrams."

"I had the same requirements, assignments and tests for all students and expected the same of you as any student taking the introductory course." Jonas had this memorized. He'd stood his ground then and would do so now. "Which, by the way, was a very general and *very* easy course."

"Fuck was it, motherfucker!" Braydon yelled.

"What is going *on* here?" came a new voice a second before the pastor came into view. "This is a house of God and—" He stopped dead at the sight before him.

"Sir…" Rye got his attention and showed his badge. "I'm taking care of this—please step aside."

The pastor backed away, not taking his eyes from them until he'd rounded the corner again and vanished from sight.

"Do you know how much my life went to shit because of you?" Braydon's eyes looked too small in his face as he spat the words out. "You remember Brittany? No? Ashley? No? Well, doesn't matter—they couldn't run far away from me quick enough once I wasn't playing. All the girls did."

"You're married." Rye nodded at the wedding band Braydon wore.

The yelling and screaming this provoked told anyone in earshot of Braydon's feelings for Kayleigh, his wife back in his hometown, and her father, in whose store Braydon worked, and the loss of his one big chance, his ticket out. "I could have been in the fucking AHL," he cried. "The scouts came to college, and I know they were interested in me, would have wanted me, but they didn't see me play, not when I was benched from the Terrell Tigers for those games because of my grades!"

"I don't know anything about the situation, or the college, but I'm pretty damn sure there was stuff to help students catch up, especially athletes with potential. Like, extra classes or reading or the material written out in a simpler way, or even one-on-one tutoring." Rye folded his arms. "I'm not seeing how this is the professor's fault."

"Yeah, you're right. You don't know nothing about it, or your sweet, moral little Professor Abrams."

The sly, vindictive twist to Braydon's features warned Jonas of what was coming. *Shit. No. Not again.* Braydon wasn't the hunk he'd been back then, back when he'd played to perfection the naïve country boy whose physique and potential had brought him to the big city, but he'd been credible enough then and —

"He's a fucking fag!" Braydon screamed. "One who said he'd made my grade low so he'd give me a higher one if I sucked his dick and fucked him in the ass!"

His words rang out, hitting Jonas as they had back then, but before the full weight struck, before the echoes even faded, Rye laughed.

"You lying piece of shit. How the fuck did anyone ever believe that crap?"

"They didn't. Not exactly. The department told me off the record they knew he must be lying, but they asked me to step down while they 'looked into it' so they covered their own backs." It still hurt. "I stepped down, for the rest of the semester, and after the summer break, my contract wasn't renewed."

"So you were fired, it boiled down to, over this?" Rye looked disgusted.

"Good! You fucking deserve it!" Braydon screamed, literally screamed, long and primal and wordless, revealing the extent of his mental health issues.

"Braydon, you need help and if you are getting help, you need more, or different help," Jonas said, hurting despite himself for this man who remained fixated on one past incident that had ruined his entire life and its prospects and also how he saw the world. Wait — that sounded familiar.

His concern swung into fear when Braydon moved toward him. Before he'd taken two steps, Rye was there, restraining him, pinning his arms behind his back and slamming him over the trunk of the car. Sirens blared on the road.

"Who called the police?" Jonas asked, wondering if Rye had some sort of law enforcement button he pressed to summon his fellow officers.

"I did." The pastor crept around the side of the church again. "And I recorded what happened."

Jonas was glad about that, when he had to explain to the cops. It sounded so crazy, fantastic even, and yet it was true, was happening.

"You best get a restraining order against this whack job," one of the cops advised, after listening to Braydon admit that he regularly googled Jonas' name and so knew he was on a radio program, to which he'd listened, and learned where Jonas worked, so he'd staked out the area and stalked him.

Jonas thanked the police officers. "I'll put it on my to-do list," he muttered, trying not to tremble.

Chapter Seventeen

"C'mere." As soon as they were alone, Rye took Jonas' shivering body in his arms and just held him, tight and hard. "That's solved now, darlin'," he crooned, rubbing Jonas' back. "You can breathe easier. No more hang-up calls." He hated that Jonas had been put through this. Was still going through this.

Rye could understand why Jonas had cut himself off from people of his own background. And hadn't his partner left him over the accusation and Jonas being fired in all but name too? No wonder he preferred one-night stands when he needed to get laid.

Except...Rye wasn't that, was he? What they had...well, Rye didn't understand it, but felt it, and hoped Jonas did too. Jonas' looks had made Rye's breath catch in his throat when he'd first seen him, those big, intelligent brown eyes, narrowing in thought or concentration, widening in admiration. And the clever, funny, defiant man behind the looks was the cake. Or the icing. Whatever. Rye wasn't smart like Jonas. All he knew was it was all good.

"Feelin' okay to drive, sugar?" he asked, the endearment slipping out.

Jonas nodded. "I've missed a department meeting, but I can't miss the class I'm teaching and I don't want to."

"So come on." Rye tailed close behind Jonas for the remainder of the journey and parked in one of the faculty spots. The doctor it belonged to wasn't using it. He looked around the campus, getting his bearings. It was cleverly laid out from north to south gateway, all landscaped trees and paths and spots with benches or grass between the buildings, encouraging walking and making the most of the space without it feeling too cramped.

"That's the library." Jonas pointed to the pale stone and glass building in the distance. "I didn't think before, but they have small study rooms you can book that are private and soundproofed. You have a laptop, don't you? It shouldn't be too difficult to get a landline to plug in and a printer or scanner or whatever you need. Should I come with you?"

It should be Rye accompanying Jonas, who still looked a little pale, and why wouldn't he? But the thought of a private room, rather than the department office or lounge where he could be overheard, swayed Rye. "Go," he ordered Jonas, who was looking at the time on his watch. He slapped him on the ass to speed him on his way.

Inside the library, Rye didn't commandeer a phone, or even use his. He still needed to lay everything out, make sure all the facts were correct and the incidents in the right order, including today's involving Lina. Oh, that stung. Had she been involved, when Chip was alive? Had she been the one to force him into things, even? Rye shook his head. He preferred to think the cartel had approached her after, to discourage her from digging into her husband's finances and holdings, perhaps, or from raising any questions about them if she'd already found anything, making her powerless to do anything but obey. He was extra careful as he wrote that event up.

The alarm he'd set on his phone beeped, startling him. Huh. He was never jumpy. *Guess I was really concentrating.* He packed his stuff away, hurrying because he'd arranged to meet Jonas at the entrance after his class. Put like that, it made him smile. *Like we're high school sweethearts, stealing a few moments together in between classes*, with Rye sneaking over after shop and Jonas fresh from some advanced placement stuff or other.

The thought would make Jonas smile too. Rye would tell him, as soon as he saw him, if not here inside the vestibule—Rye peered around—then outside the main entrance, on the steps. Only...Jonas wasn't there either. Okay, his class ran over, Rye forced himself to think, to believe, but couldn't make himself not have that feeling of ice water trickling down his spine. That threat to Jonas was over, that crazy bastard who'd been calling him and hanging up, probably trailing him for days, was over, so why did Rye feel—?

No. He felt nothing. Jonas had...a history emergency. *Really, Ryland?* he mocked himself. He forced himself to wait, then tensed when someone headed for him.

"Hi there!" The blonde running up the steps seemed to get extra bouncy as she neared him. "You look a little lonely...I mean *lost*, there? Need any company...I mean *help*?" She licked her lips.

"I'm waiting for someone," Rye answered curtly. "Thanks anyway," he added.

"Are you a professor?" she continued, coming right up to him.

"No." The thought was laughable.

"Oh. Pity." She tossed her hair over her shoulder. "Because I bet you could teach *me* a thing or two."

It couldn't be that week near the beginning of the academic year where students did dares and pulled pranks. Rye had had women coming on to him before, of course, but hadn't expected it here, for some reason, or someone so brazen. He had to smile at how forward the girl was, and she winked as she made her way inside.

Feeling like a fish out of water made Rye wonder if he actually was in the wrong place. He waited a minute, to make sure the blonde didn't think he was chasing after her like a dog after the butcher's van, then walked back in. "Excuse me," he called to the young woman, maybe a college student, behind the first information desk. "Is there another door? An entrance, I mean? I'm meeting someone and they didn't show."

"Where are they coming from?" the girl asked.

"History department."

"Then the main entrance there would be the logical one. There are emergency exits, of course, and an unofficial smokers' patio off to the side." She pointed, then perhaps seeing in his face that that wasn't likely, continued, "And they meant this library? Not the one inside the department?"

Of course! It had to be! Rye thanked her and grabbed a printed map from a stand. He waited another minute outside, shading his eyes to peer in one direction after another, and when there was still no Jonas in sight, jogged off. He called Jonas' phone as he went. It rang but no one picked up and it went to voice mail.

"Oh, er, hi. It's Rye." He grimaced. He hated these fuckin' things. "I guess I got the wrong meeting place? If you get this and you're at the library inside your department, stay there, okay?"

The last thing he wanted was he and Jonas crisscrossing plazas and lawns or going into and out of buildings or racing through archways all over this campus and missing each other at every turn, like some goddamn comedy movie. The shortcut he took brought him near to the car park they'd used earlier.

"Maybe we said meet at the cars," he said to no one and not even convincing himself, but he needed to hear something else apart from his own heartbeat that was starting to thunder in his ears. Well, it would—his heart was beating so hard it was knocking against his ribs. He took in a deep breath and let it out.

Their vehicles were there, with no brown-haired, glasses-wearing professor waiting by them. There was no reason Jonas should have been there, but his absence added another note to the alarms ringing and trying to become deafening. No—Rye wouldn't let them. He called Jonas' phone again...and it was answered. "Oh, thank fuck," Rye breathed. "Jonas—"

The call was cut off. Cursing, Rye pressed Redial. "The person you are trying to reach is currently not available," announced a tinny voice.

"The hell?" Rye gulped. That meant the phone was switched off, didn't it? Why would Jonas— *Well, maybe he got called into some last-minute meeting with his boss, or co-workers. They'd switch off their cells not to be disturbed.*

So Rye would go wait for him there. It sounded reasonable, so why was he thumping his fist down on Jonas' stupid little car in frustration and fear?

"Sir?"

Rye turned at the man's voice. *Kid's voice*, he corrected himself, eyeing the young guy in his pale blue shorts and darker blue polo, lanyard around his neck and badge pinned to his shirt. "What? Well? And make it quick, boy," he advised.

"May I ask what you're doing at the staff vehicles, sir? I know you're not Dr. Kramer, Department Chair, History."

"I'm not...? Oh." The guy—or woman—whose parking spot Rye had taken, or so the sign told him. He looked from it back to the nervous security guard. "True. Kid, I'm reaching for my ID, okay?" He waited for the guy to nod understanding before flashing him his badge. The guard's eyes widened. "And I need to get to the history department right now."

"I'll take you!" the kid offered. "Oh, wait. I have to supervise the puppy program at the enclosure on South Lawn. Take my vehicle." He stepped aside, revealing a golf cart. "It's a utility vehicle!"

"No offense, kid, but it ain't. *That's* a utility vehicle." Rye patted his Ford. "What's your top speed, eighteen mph? I can *run* faster."

He headed off, doing just that, the kid's "I've gotten it up to twenty before!" trailing after him. He was almost glad for the interruption as a relief from his thoughts, but not for the delay.

"Jonas Abrams?" he demanded of whoever was around in the small building he stormed into. "Professor Abrams?"

"Sir…" A woman barging out of her office quietened down at the sight of his badge. "Try the faculty lounge?" She indicated the way.

Jonas wasn't sitting there, sipping coffee or tea, having forgotten about their meeting when Rye burst in. "I'm looking for Jonas Abrams," Rye said, holding his badge out like a talisman and raking each person there with his gaze. "He had a class—he teach it?"

"He did," a woman confirmed, walking in from whatever room was through the far doorway. "I have the carrel next to the one he uses and his books and notes are there."

Not asking permission and ignoring the mutters and even the questions being asked of him, Rye raced through to some study or prep room, when he grabbed at a bag on one of the small desks. Yeah, it was Jonas'. Rye rifled through it, finding nothing that helped explain. "So he left this after his class? Have you seen him since he finished it?"

"No. Or before. Sorry." The woman didn't look sorry. "He hasn't been here long, and he has one foot here and one in art history, you know?"

Did she mean he should check there?

"And he left his previous post, in Dallas, suddenly," she continued. "He was on track for tenure but just walked out, I heard. So maybe…" She spread her hands, her meaning obvious, that Jonas had taken a hike from here too.

"Or maybe you could stop flapping your gums about things you don't know shit about," Rye interrupted. He waited for her to look ashamed and drop her eyes before he left. He tried the small library here and the meeting rooms, all in vain, before exiting the building and heading back to the car park, not knowing what else to do.

When he reached his truck, he pressed Redial…and the phone was answered. Relief flooded him, making him sag against his vehicle. "Jonas! Where—?"

The man's voice that answered wasn't Jonas'. Instead, it was one from straight out of a nightmare.

"Jonas can't come to the phone right now. He's tied to a chair," it mocked, then added, "Jonas, be a good boy and say hi to your Ranger buddy."

Rye's breath stuck in his throat, unable to exit over the huge lump suddenly there. "*Jonas.*"

"Rye? Rye, don't do what they say. Don't listen to them—" Jonas' words were cut off by a meaty thwack, a hand striking flesh, and ended in a cry of pain.

"To whoever is listening, you should know this." Rye swallowed, needing his voice level and deadly. "I'm gonna track down every last one of you pieces of shit and—"

"Every threat you make," crooned the man's voice, to the tune of an old song. "Every step you take…we take it out of your boyfriend's ass." The singsong stopped. "Not literally. *Paneleiros* makes me sick." He spat. Physically spat. "Now, this is normally the part where we say don't call in the cops or…well, you can supply the threat. But with you, there's no need, right? You won't. So just sit tight and don't do anything stupid, *entendido*?"

The call was cut, and Rye swore. Long and loud, and he didn't realize he'd gotten into his truck until he started banging his fists on the steering wheel. Then, when he knew what he was doing, he couldn't stop, not until he drew blood. He switched to banging his head instead. Just once, then twice. He started the engine, not knowing where he was going until he headed for his motel room.

Inside, he stopped and thought. Took a long, hard look at things. At himself. Those bastards who had Jonas had said Rye wouldn't call in the cops. Jonas' words came back to him. *"You prefer to deal with things alone? You don't trust other people?"*

Jonas wasn't the only one to call him some variation on the Lone Ranger, and that wasn't totally incorrect. Rye did rely on himself, He'd had to, just as his younger sister had had to rely on him after their parents' deaths. *"You always think you have to be the one who handles everything, don't you?"* Lina had hissed at him.

He did, and he'd been reluctant to take this to anyone else. Not knowing who to trust was only part of the reason. He faced that now. He didn't have to do this alone. *I can't. Not when Jonas is in danger.* The thought of life without him —

Rye took out the spare chip he'd bought for his burner phone and inserted it, calling his boss, Lt. LeGrande, his senior captain, Chief Fischer and the Waco headquarters captain, Assistant Chief Pereira. At the same time, he sent them all the email he'd finished composing, laying everything out.

He finished and put his first chip back into his cell. It buzzed a message — a photo. He frowned at it for a second before understanding that it was of a bloodstained watch. A watch Rye recognized. He opened the message that had come after it.

Next time, a finger.

The next photo to arrive was of a pair of smashed glasses. Like the watch, he knew those too. This message was even worse.

Next time, an eye.

Every inch of Rye was ice-cold with horror. Then the next message that arrived sent red-hot heat burning in him. Not because it read, *Wanna join the party?*

Because it contained an address.

Fuck yeah, Rye wanted to party. He'd get his best gear on for it.

Chapter Eighteen

Rye double-checked the address. Whatever he'd been expecting when he reached the outskirts of San Antonio, it wasn't *this*. "Here?" he said again, as he had when he'd left his truck in the parking garage. He blinked under the bright lighting and skylights that shone on the escalators, elevators and stairways and picked out the lurid signs announcing sales in the stores. "*A shopping mall?*"

"Enjoy, sir," a pastel-uniformed man said, gesturing with one hand as Rye passed him.

"What? What did you just say to me?" Rye narrowed his eyes at the guy, his hand going for his Sig.

"Excuse me?" the man replied, bewildered, then turned to a trio of women entering the store he stood outside and made the same hand flourish. "Have a great shopping experience, ladies!"

Oh, for fuck's sake. Rye's heart rate slowed a little. The idiot was some greeter outside of a stupid store. He had to stop thinking every single person—and there were lots, carrying bags, pushing baby strollers and browsing storefront windows — was a cartel member, ready to pick him off. No, this was a checkpoint, so they could tell he was alone, not leading a team to back him up, as much as he wished that were the case.

He wandered past a line of kiosks staffed by women with more makeup on their faces than they had on their counters and turned right, down a quieter corridor. Was he supposed to go into the shops? This area held banks, travel stores and a goddamn dry cleaner, as far as he could see.

He turned back into the bigger main area and took out his cell phone. The only thing he could think of doing was to call Jonas' number, as much as it hurt to think of Jonas not being able to pick up, because of what those bastards might be doing to him. Christ, he'd make them pay.

He'd relayed this latest development to LeGrande, Fischer and Pereira, too. If they weren't all in on this, they should be sending reinforcements. Until then, he was on his own.

"I'm here, you fuckers," he growled into his phone when it was answered.

"*Tsk*. That's not nice," the voice from earlier reproved. "Now —"

"Now I speak to Jonas, before this — whatever the fuck it is — goes any further. That's non-negotiable," Rye interrupted, his voice ringing with steel.

The muffled silence suggested to Rye that this was being discussed, maybe through a hierarchy, and he prepared to wait.

"Rye?"

Rye closed his eyes. He'd expected some comeback to his demand, some terms to be thrashed out, not

Jonas' voice on the other end of the line. "Y'all okay?" he rasped.

"Yes." He didn't sound that okay, not to Rye, who was familiar with the nuances of his speech, even after knowing him for such a short time. "Are *you* okay?" Jonas continued.

"Me? Oh, I'm just peachy," Rye snarled. "Raring to go. Get ready, because I'll be with you soon."

As soon as he could, for all he was stalling, giving the Waco HQ time to mobilize. The Rangers had a field office here. It shouldn't be that difficult.

"Go to the end of the short corridor," the Hispanic voice ordered.

"Oh? Need me to pick up your dry cleaning? You too fuckin' lazy?" Poking the bear was stupid, but Rye did it anyway.

"The other short corridor, *cabrón*."

Bristling at the insult, another thing to be avenged, Rye crossed to the other side of the main area and turned down the smaller corridor there. He walked slowly, waiting for more instructions as he passed expensive specialty stores, their windows displaying hand-rolled cigars, artisan chocolates and embroidered purses, but nothing else was relayed, and he came out of the other end, into the place's food court.

"Explore the sights," the man on the phone told him. "You'll be given instructions."

"Hey, moron, just because you've seen *Dirty Harry* a few too many times don't mean I—" Rye cursed as the call was cut. He turned in a slow circle, taking in the burger places, coffee houses, smoothie bars and ice cream outlets.

"Don't people have frozen yogurt anymore?" he muttered. *Actually, fuck froyo.* He should be glad there weren't *payphones* anymore. At least he was spared that part of the movie re-enactment. Was he supposed to select a specific bench where his contact would be? No one looked up from their phones to tell him, if so.

He sniffed the grilling meat and herbed tomato scents of food cooking. Jesus, he was hungry. His cell buzzed.

Lava Java. Be nice.

The fuck? Well, the name was that of the coffee place right there, with a circular counter set around the espresso or whatever machines and cash register. Be nice meant get talking? To whoever would give him the real location? He joined the short line. "The coffee good here?" he asked the guy in front of him.

The guy swung around. "Its ratio is good," he replied, shoving his phone almost in Rye's face. "Got five beans on Silver Spoon, four and half cups on DrinkMe and, see—"

"Yeah. I get it." *God. This generation. Guy probably has to read the reviews to know what to order.* Rye got a black coffee and moved around the counter a little, nearly spilling his overpriced drink when his phone buzzed.

I said be nice.

"Fuck you," Rye muttered, hoping they could hear.

A teenage girl just along from him looked up from under her ink-black curtain of hair.

"Not you," Rye assured her, supposing she'd heard. "I mean, I wasn't—"

"Yeah, so, don't hit on me?" she said, cutting across whatever he'd been trying to say. Tossing her fall of hair over one shoulder, she dropped her plastic cup on the floor and walked away.

"*Kids.*" A janitor started to bend down with a grunt, his hand outstretched for the cup. "Hope that was empty. If not I gotta…"

Rye wasn't listening. Not when the young girl turned and stared at him, her black-eyeliner-rimmed gaze cool as she dragged it down his body…to the plastic cup. "Wait!" he ordered the old guy who was about to drop the cup into his garbage sack. "I need that."

"Welcome to it." Shaking his head, the janitor held it out, tsking as Rye snatched it…to read the two words written on the side. At big coffee outlets, the baristas wrote the clients' names on the cups, making it easy for them to get the right drink at the other end of the station. These words, however, weren't anyone's name. They were instructions.

Parking garage.

Rye's heart thudded. He'd passed their tests? Met their requirements in walking about here like an idiot, so they knew he was alone? His boots clapping on the tile floor, he hurried from the mall, back the way he'd come, happy enough to leave the skylights and bright colors for the low roof and gray concrete pillars of the garage, as discomforting and claustrophobic as it was.

And where a handful of maintenance guys, all wearing generic brown coveralls and not branded ones of the mall or a third-party service company, hung about. A normal-enough sight in a parking garage maybe, but none of these men were working on anything specific, and nothing that required specialized tools or equipment.

Jonas wouldn't be held here. *Shit.* There would be a storage area within the garage, but no way would a cartel be using it. It wasn't big enough to be a storehouse for product, much less to do any repackaging needed before it was sent on to the next stage of its journey deeper into the state. Rye hadn't really expected this to be the destination of *his* journey, but still, *shit.*

Rye counted up the number of these 'service personnel' standing around doing nothing in particular. Could be the guys were all on break? *Yeah, right.* He weighed up the odds and calculated them as shit, too. He gave it five minutes, but no further messages came and Jonas' phone rang unanswered when Rye called it. Then like a signal, the section of lights in the lane where he'd left his Ford went out, leaving it in a patch of darker grayness. *Okay. More than one way to send a message.*

He walked to his truck, his skin prickling at the feeling of being observed. He wasn't followed — there was no need. Rye got into his vehicle on high alert and within a minute, he was jerking his head from side to side to watch men approaching. The one who reached the driver's side knocked on the window and made universal 'roll this down' signs.

Rye preferred to open his door instead, and two of the men pulled him out. Now the crew was all teamwork and efficiency, two patting him down and the rest searching his truck. He doubted they'd find his Colt AR-15 stashed away and he was right. The guy who pushed him against the side of his Ford and patted him down stripped him of his Sig, then laughed on finding his smaller backup pocket pistol. He took that too.

"Small size, eh?" the guy jeered, getting quips back from the rest of the men about 'performance'.

Rye didn't respond. He was focused on discerning as many features of the gang as he could, seeking anything that stood out and would help him identify them, as hard as that was when they all wore ballcaps pulled low on their foreheads.

"You got a good memory, *tombo*?" one asked.

The one who reached me first. The boss of this gang. Rye cataloged the man's taller-than-average height and resulting slight stoop, filing that away next to the damaged fingers on the left hand of the man who'd searched him, and the scarred neck of a third guy. He nodded in answer to the question.

With a, "You better," his questioner rattled off an address. "Head for the Hill Country. You'll find it." He patted the driver's seat and gave a tilt of his head at the truck's cabin.

Having expected to be taken to the secondary location, more than probably blindfolded and in the trunk of a vehicle not his own, Rye fought to conceal his surprise.

The tall guy snorted. "What do you think, amigos?" he asked his men. "He needs a guide, huh?"

This got more laughs. Tall Guy whistled and a click-clack noise reached Rye's ears a second before a large dark brown Doberman pinscher walked up and stood in their midst. It had to stand thirty inches high and weigh a hundred pounds, all of it muscle. Its black body and tan face were familiar to Rye, although when he'd seen the animal before, it had been lying down and barely looked at him. On its feet, staring hard at him, it was a different story.

At a command, the dog jumped into the passenger seat, its spring one of controlled power.

"He'll take you right to the boss." Bad Hand Guy smirked hard. "Just try not to shit your pants, yeah? Pablo don't like that."

Rye was scared, but more about what could be happening to Jonas than sharing the cabin of his truck with a dog that was clearly well trained. The breed was used by the armed services and was a personal defense dog and a war dog, but this one was quiet and almost contemplative, making his company soothing rather than nerve-wracking. Rye loved dogs, anyhow.

"So, your name's Pablo? We weren't introduced when I saw you before." Rye glanced at him, and the dog flicked him half a glance. "Well, as much as you should be in the back with a harness attached to the seat belt, I guess you won't be, right?" He kept his hand slow as he programmed the address he'd been given into the GPS, making no sudden movements. A Doberman's bite pressure was off-the-charts hard.

"Friend of mine had a Dobie," Rye informed Pablo, his eyes on the road now. "I remember him calling him 'sleek but substantial'. He used to snap tennis balls in half with one bite. I'd love to pet you, especially if you're helping me get to Jonas."

Jonas. Who must be so scared, squinting at his surroundings without his glasses, his thick brown hair mussed. Rye didn't let himself dwell on what other privations Jonas must be going through. He thought instead of when he'd first seen him, those brown eyes gleaming with intelligence and focus, and of their first fuck, Jonas' full lips issuing commands and, on their next meetings, dropping sass. Rye had liked each facet he'd discovered, from Jonas' brains to his bravado, his passions to his…preferences. They had something real between them, and Rye wanted it to grow.

"I'll get you home, sugar," he whispered. *Promised.* "And they'll pay a hundred times over for what they did to you."

Pablo lifted his head, his eyes front.

"We're here?" Rye slowed, driving through a gap in the chain link fencing and pulling up to the location. An old canning plant, or so its sign said. "Yeah, guess a processing plant would be too much." The product already came cut and dried.

"You got manners," Rye told Pablo when the dog waited calmly for Rye to go around and open his door. "I like that. Wish I had a treat for ya. But I guess you don't snack when you're on duty?"

Because it was clear the Doberman was working, leading Rye to a side door in one of the large corrugated-metal buildings that had giant delivery bays in the back. "Let me get that for you," Rye said, pushing at the heavy door, although he bet Pablo could open it. The metallic squeal the door gave set Rye's teeth on edge, and the old, sour smell of the open warehouse space within had his nose wrinkling.

There were no painted lines marking out walking paths, but Pablo didn't need them, taking Rye past rusty shelving and rotting pallets and an assembly line to a packaging center at the back that would be handy for the transport bays outside.

"Pablo!" A guy cheered the dog, and Rye recognized the man from the card club, just as he remembered the next man, clapping for Pablo, from the bar at the pool hall. He thought, although he couldn't swear to it, that he recalled a third from the fair.

"Who's next, the pastor from church? The head of the university?" he muttered as the group of men grew. Pablo walked past them and vanished into the back somewhere, and Rye faced them all.

"I wanna see Jonas," he said.

One of the men, the pool place guy, gave a quick glance upward. "He's right here," he snarked a second later, and the half-circle parted to let Rye see Jonas in the alcove behind them, tied to a chair, his face bloody.

There was so much Rye wanted to say, so many emotions racing through him, but, surrounded as he and Jonas were, and *where* they were, all he could do was ask, "Y'all okay?"

"What do you think?" Jonas retorted. "I hate having my photograph taken…"

Rye followed the slight movement of Jonas' head and noticed a video camera and laptop.

"Livestreaming," Pool Hall Owner said. He'd taken the lead when Rye was there, and Rye had thought at the time the guy was probably the owner as well as the manager. "For training purposes." He sniggered. "And a warning, maybe, if things go…"

He used an expression that meant something like 'all the way', and Rye understood. If they executed Jonas, and presumably him too.

"Doesn't have to be like that." Pool Hall Owner seemed to guess Rye's thoughts. He gave another tiny glance upward. "Could even work out good for you. We got plenty cops on staff." He sniggered again and jerked his thumb over his shoulder to one guy, who gave an embarrassed shrug.

Rye felt a flicker of recognition, although he didn't know from where. "You make a good case," he replied, hoping his reading of the situation, the dynamics, was correct. "But I don't like dealing with monkeys."

This got gasps and curses, and even a gob of spit aimed at him.

"You mean flunkies?" Jonas asked.

"*Monkeys*. As in, I wanna speak to the organ grinder." Jonas raised his voice and tipped his head back to look up at the metal observation platform over the assembly room floor, where Pool Hall Guy had been looking for permission or approval.

Silence stretched for a moment then footsteps indicated someone was walking along, to descend the metal stairway to their left. The footsteps weren't dull boot thuds, and the someone wasn't a man. The steps were quick and the sound was one of high heels clicking…and their owner the woman he'd taken to be a bartender in Nieves Tacos.

"The organ grinder?" the woman repeated. She was a lot more expensively dressed now, and her jewelry flashed and shone. Her glossy lips twisted in a mean smile seconds before she grabbed the crotch of the man nearest to her and cupped, squeezing and twisting hard and for long enough to bring tears to his eyes and have his knees shaking. She let out a humorless laugh. "That's one of my nicknames, *sí*."

Chapter Nineteen

Rye's here! He'd come for Jonas, as he promised, and Jonas felt equal parts relief at that and fear for Rye, at being here too...mixed in with a little anger that if it weren't for Rye, *Jonas* wouldn't be here. No. That wasn't helpful. Rye was here, with a plan to get them out. Jonas stared at him, trying to discern what steps were in place for their rescue, but Rye gave nothing away...so much so that Jonas, who knew Rye's expressions and how good his poker face...wasn't, closed his eyes at the fear swamping him again.

No. Jonas forced his eyes open. He wouldn't think like that, wouldn't lump Rye in with all the other people who'd said comforting, meaningless words to him then let him be thrown to the wolves so they could keep the flock, or the Ivory Towers, nice and safe. Rye wasn't like Ben, happy to sacrifice Jonas when it was expedient to do so, and neither was Jonas some pathetic idiot who couldn't do anything to help himself. He'd use the abilities he had to hand, ones he'd honed over years of practice.

He could usually read situations, even dicey ones when adrenaline coursed through him, but now, with the arrival of this person on whom he should be focusing, and not Rye, he was finding it hard to pay attention and discern.

Of course, he wasn't usually in this much fear for his life. Or aching from being tied to a chair. He'd been surprised to learn that abductors actually did that, or still did that, to their victims. He tried to gauge the men's reactions as the woman descended from on high to stalk among them, her mane of hair swishing with her rapid movements.

So *this* was who all the sidelong glances and bitten-off whispers among the men had been about? Jonas knew enough Spanish to understand that the men were expecting an arrival, some big boss or VIP. He wished he had his glasses—he had a spare pair in his pocket as always—but didn't expect anyone would fish them out and settle them on his face for him.

The woman from the tacos place! He'd thought at the time she was more than a bar keep, but seeing her now, like this, he wondered just how high up in the organization she was. Everything about her, from her walk to her clothes to her posture, screamed power. Rye must be picking up on that, too. Did it change the plans he had in motion?

"In addition to that," the woman said, coming close to peer at Jonas, so close that the patchouli scent of her perfume smothered him, "I'm also known as The Snow Angel."

"Snow as in Nieves, your surname?" Rye asked.

A few of the men laughed.

"That's one reason," the woman agreed. "My name's Antonella—people call me Angelita."

She didn't look like a little angel. Anyone who called her that was trying to flatter her.

"*The Angel*," Rye repeated, as if solving a puzzle.

Antonella preened. "You heard of me! And you're surprised because I'm a woman?" She frowned at Rye, as if detecting that he'd moved a step or two — he had — and gestured at her men to crowd closer, so they stood nearer to both his right and left sides, and behind him too.

"I'm surprised how far you've climbed the ladder," Jonas replied, drawing their attention.

"You shut your filthy mouth!" one of the men cried, approaching Jonas with his hand out, ready to strike.

"Stop," Antonella ordered, and her flunky did.

Jonas was grateful — Rye had been poised to retaliate, or strike first, and a huge meaty-handed man grabbed him from behind to pin his arms to his body.

"You know who I am?" Antonella stared so hard at Jonas through her heavily made-up dark eyes that he felt she was burning two holes in him and seeing right into his soul.

"Not exactly. But I see you're someone who's worked hard to get where you are. Harder than a man would have to," Jonas answered.

"You're right." Antonella made a half-turn to look at her men. "He's right. I know what you think — what you believe — but I wasn't born into narco royalty."

"But your father..." started the man from the pool hall. He was the highest-ranking of the men, the one closest to Antonella. Jonas could tell that because he was the only one armed.

"Wasn't that high up in the Camargo." Antonella's smile held contempt, perhaps for her father or perhaps for the people she had fooled. Jonas wasn't sure. "Luis

Guerrero was a street-level distributor who just happened to be useful to Alfonso Carrillo."

Even Jonas had heard of that name. Carrillo was a wanted man, a cartel leader. Wasn't he on the run?

"Useful because of *me*. I looked like his daughter enough to become her body double, her human shield, and my father was taken on as her bodyguard. It was a good life."

"Yeah!" one of the idiots cheered.

"Swim classes, ballet, horse riding, language lessons, sharpshooting..." Briefly misty-eyed, she turned to Jonas. "Do you know how old I was when I witnessed my first shootout?"

Jonas thought. "Twelve?"

She looked impressed. "Thirteen. That's when I became full-time cartel, learning all I could, making all the connections I could to rise through the ranks."

Rye shifted where he stood, and Jonas knew what he was thinking. He too wanted to ask, "*Is there a point to this?*" but in every movie or TV series he'd ever seen in which there was some situation like this, the victim had kept the captor talking.

"What happened then?" he asked. "I can tell something went wrong." Because if she'd simply been handed the keys to the kingdom as a matter of course, she wouldn't be jangling them. Well, jangling so much gaudy gold jewelry, but it meant the same.

"The Sandoval Brothers killed her one day, in broad daylight. So Carrillo killed my father." Antonella shrugged. "And kicked me out onto the streets. I was on my own. And women in this world are seen as objects or a reward or a necessity, but not as someone with ideas and dreams and the skills and determination to make those dreams a reality. Not a real person."

"You look pretty real to me," Jonas said.

"Real enough to start right at the bottom." Striking suddenly, like a snake, she grabbed Jonas' face in one hand, squashing it and digging her nails in. "Not like you, Mr. Fancy College Teacher. You're clever, *si*? So, do you know what a *halcone* is, *profesor*?"

"It means falcon, doesn't it?" Jonas, scared and uncomfortable, made himself sound interested.

"*Muy bueno*." Antonella slid her hand free and patted Jonas' face, the force she used making it nearer to a slap. "Yeah, falcons are the lowest rank, the eyes and ears on the street, keeping watch for cops or rivals, and reporting it back. And now..." She preened.

Now you have all this, Jonas didn't say while casting a rolling-eyed glance around the filthy abandoned factory. He wanted to, though. But she presumably ran a very lucrative supply chain or route for the cocaine, or snow. It was a shame that her name wasn't Reina or Regina. Then she could have been known as the Snow Queen.

She snapped her fingers and the corrupt cop stood to attention. "*La bolsa*," she ordered him, and he shot up the stairs to retrieve her purse then stood holding the compact she passed him, so she could see to refresh her lipstick.

"The camera," she explained, pointing an elbow at it. "I have to look good, in case we're filming more..."

And crap. Being filmed while being mocked and slapped about earlier had been bad enough. He'd been promised...worse.

"What do you want?" Antonella asked suddenly, dropping her makeup into her fringed purse and handing it back to her dirty-cop ladies' maid.

"Want?" Jonas didn't know what she meant.

"I could kill both of you now, but it would bring heat to us." She sounded like she was discussing takeout choices for dinner. *Chinese is less carb-laden than pizza but has more sodium. Hm. What to select...* And it meant she must have bought Rye's story, that killing him would release his story far and wide. Or maybe it wasn't a lie. Rye could have put that failsafe in place.

"So I ask you again, what do you want?" Antonella tapped a toe.

"Really? To not be here," Jonas answered.

"Miguel."

The sharp order had Antonella's second-in-command punching Jonas in the stomach for that answer.

"I don't want to ruin my acrylics," Antonella explained, shooting a fleeting tight-lipped smile in thanks to the gorilla-like flunky who kept Rye from moving. "Last chance..." She snapped her fingers at Jonas this time.

"I don't know!" Jonas wheezed. Except he did, because it hit him as suddenly as Miguel's fist had. *Rye.* He wanted Rye. Wanted the chance to get to know him more deeply, to discover if they were as compatible as Jonas thought...if they could make a life together, even. What an inappropriate time to get such a revelation. But it wasn't a revelation. Not really. Jonas thought he'd known from the start. Had Rye?

"Clock's ticking."

Antonella's tap of her long-nailed finger on her wrist brought Jonas back to the present. He wouldn't talk about Rye. That was private. "What I want? I've always wanted to be a tenured professor. Maybe...to write a bestselling history textbook? No — to design a course exactly the way I want it and to teach it, have students enroll at the college because of it. Or maybe..." *To write.* He'd already mentioned textbooks, but he didn't mean academic works or nonfiction at all.

"Enough." Antonella shook her head at him. "It's not a quiz. There's no right answer." She paused for her flunkies to laugh. "And you, *tombo*?"

It was a slur used for a cop. If nothing else, Jonas' Spanish slang had improved after a few hours here.

"Me? That's easy. To see y'all answering for your crimes." Rye's answer came pat and was a better one, Jonas acknowledged.

Antonella stalked toward him and grabbed his face as she had Jonas'. It seemed to be her go-to move and, recalling how she'd grabbed one of her men lower down, Jonas was glad for it. She studied Rye. "Last chance to take a bribe. Santiago, *la maleta*."

That junior hopped off, returning with a suitcase. At his boss' finger-click he fumbled it open to display its contents like he was a model on a game show, and Jonas gasped at the bank notes it contained.

"That can't be real!" he burst out. He was ignored.

"This money is untraceable," Antonella started.

Rye shook his head. "Anyone who works in law enforcement will tell you there ain't no such thing as untraceable banknotes, ma'am."

"Fine." She nodded at her assistant to close the case and bear it away. "So you agree to call off your vendetta, to turn a blind eye to the transport?"

"What? Why the hell would I do that?" Rye demanded, sounding as confused as Jonas felt.

"Because if not, I'll have your friend here killed." She pointed at Jonas. "Either now or at any time in the future. Think about that." Rye didn't seem to be giving her the reaction she wanted, and this made her sigh, as if she were talking to an idiot. "You're in love with him."

The words she spat out next, her opinion of the LGBTI community, would have gotten her fired from most places of work, or at the very least sent for sensitivity and inclusivity training. Then what she'd said registered, and Jonas had trouble breathing. He stared at Rye. "You *love* me?"

Rye stared back, saying nothing, but Jonas supplied the answer for himself. *He does. He's fallen in love with me!* As if acknowledging it had made a connection between them, Jonas swore he could hear Rye thinking that if Rye said yes, it would give the cartel leverage. If he said no, he didn't love Jonas, the cartel would shoot Jonas anyway to get rid of him. They were trapped.

"Do you love me?" Rye countered instead.

And if Jonas said no, he didn't, the cartel would again shoot him anyway.

"Seems to me we're wasting time," Rye drawled, his beautiful blue eyes flashing a message.

Waste time? Stall! "Why are you asking me, and what's that look for?" Jonas snapped. "You were a great hookup, yes, I'll give you that. But anything more?" He turned to Antonella and her men. "You've studied me. Done your research. So you know my patterns. Know I enjoy a one-nighter with someone I'm not likely to run into in the daytime, in my everyday world. An easy, undemanding, unpretentious fuck." He was improvising wildly.

"That so? That all I am? Some fuckin' blue-collar pump and dump?" Rye shouted back.

Jonas scoffed. "Why are you so angry? What am I to you, some R&R while you're on assignment? Even if there was anything more between us, you made it clear your job comes first! Oh, and second and last!"

"At least I got a real job. Not just reading things out of books to kids who don't even wanna be there," Rye sniped.

"Basta!" Antonella yelled louder than both of them. "Enough! This is not cute or dorky or fun—it's giving me a headache." She exhaled. "Okay, so this was a wrong move here. One way to fix it is to kill you both. I can call in some favors I was saving, to take the heat. Santiago, get the camera working. Rafael, step forward."

She nodded when the man, the corrupt cop, did as bidden. "Miguel, throw him your gun. Time he got his precious little police officer hands dirty. Now!" she roared when Miguel hesitated.

Miguel threw his weapon to Santiago—Miguel, as her lieutenant, was the only armed man. They'd all made a big fuss about having to leave their guns in a box in the other room, but it was the rule.

This was it. There was no way out and he was going to die. Fear left Jonas ice-cold and shaking. He had so much left undone. Thoughts crowded his brain, but not of teaching and courses, the department and its strictures and demands, but of all his ideas and creativity so far untapped. His recent ideas, sparked by the exhibits. The stories he wanted to tell. And Rye. Especially Rye.

The man, gun in hand, walked forward, racking the slide like Darrell had shown Jonas. Jonas closed his eyes, then forced them open. He wouldn't die a coward. He'd stare at his murderer and—

—see him turning the gun on Antonella?

What the hell?

Chapter Twenty

"Antonella Guerrero Nieves, aka Angelita Nieves, aka The Snow Angel, you're under arrest," the man with the gun said.

Jonas' mouth fell open as the man continued, "For narcotics distribution, kidnap, unlawful detention, assault—"

"You're undercover? Pretending to be a dirty cop?" Jonas interrupted, not daring to believe. There was a way out? This was going to be okay?

"Yeah, and it sickened me." The cop broke off to shoot Jonas a glance. "Detective Rafael Gutierrez, SAPD. Friend of—"

"Darrell!" Jonas exclaimed. Now he recalled seeing this man in the small group chatting to Darrell and Aldric at the fair before the two of them came to join him and Rye.

"And building this case for a long time."

"Hey—" Rye took advantage of the confusion and alarm to pull free and leap across to Jonas. "Chat later. You got a gun for me?" He caught the small one Rafael pulled from Antonella's purse then yanked Jonas, still on his chair, deeper into the recess.

"Anyone moves, I shoot her," Rafael warned the gang…and started to walk Antonella out of there.

"What?" Jonas couldn't believe the glimpse he got of that, of the detective calmly walking out and leaving him and Rye there. He only got the briefest look because Rye was pulling tables and packing cases in front of them as a barrier.

"Don't shoot, *imbéciles*," Antonella ordered her men as she was marched out at gunpoint. "But shoot them!"

Her last words came more faintly and noises and exclamations from closer by indicated the men left behind were moving.

"They must be getting their guns!" Jonas exclaimed. He struggled to see Rye. "Untie me!"

With a grunted, "On it," Rye yanked at the ropes holding Jonas and released him. "Those knots weren't tight," he commented.

"Well, excuse me!" Jonas shook out and rubbed at his hands and feet yelping as he stretched. He tugged his spare glasses from his pocket, then went to stand, but Rye pushed him down. Before Jonas could ask why, he flinched as a bullet, then another, thudded into the table, their main shield. The bullets hit in almost the same spot, and another followed.

He'd watched enough movies to understand that the table couldn't hold together forever under such a barrage. If the men focused their firepower on a small area of the table, they'd break through it, leaving them exposed. That thought had barely formed in his mind before another bullet tore off a huge slice of wood from the top of the table. It happened so quickly he didn't register what had happened before he felt something wet on his arm. It took him twisting to stare at it then dabbing the fingers of his other hand on it to realize he was bleeding. How—?

"*Jonas?*" Rye's voice was tight.

"I'm okay." He plucked out the large sliver of wood from his upper arm, the physical pain from the injury only registering now, and bringing with it the weight of their situation. "I-I thought it was over, you know?"

"Soon will be."

Jonas didn't find Rye's words reassuring. Crouched down, he scrabbled at Rye's boot for his ankle holster gun and found it empty. *Oh no.*

"Here." Rye pulled a gun from his other boot. "Anyone searching you gives up when they find the first, you know? You use one of these?"

"It's just point and shoot, yes?"

"Yes, and now!" Rye shouted, and Jonas copied him as he turned and fired on some idiot trying to rush around the end of their barrier.

"That's for Darrell!" Jonas yelled.

"And that's pretty good shooting," Rye said.

"Darrell taught me," Jonas explained. But his hands hadn't sweated this much shooting at a big round target, and his heart hadn't thumped so hard he could hardly breathe and wanted to throw up. He twisted, in case he actually retched, and Rye yanked him back. He landed on his ass, his breath knocked out of him—just as a bullet whizzed over his head, the closest one yet. It lodged in the wall behind them, splattering plaster and drywall dust all over them. Jonas choked and coughed.

Even Rye flinched as the wooden shield in front of them was forced back an inch by the force of the bullets being pumped into it. The noise was deafening.

"Rye…" Jonas swallowed. "I think…this might be it. And if so…" What? What could he say? He stopped. "Did you hear that? Outside?" It was hard to hear over the noise inside, but something was happening. "Reinforcements, come to rescue The Snow Angel?" He and Rye were already outnumbered! Jonas could hardly think through the noise, semi darkness and the emotions churning in him. "Rye…"

"Jonas." Rye's intonation was the same as his. "I know…I guess."

"You'd better do more than *guess*," Jonas hissed, as battering from outside but near shook the ground under him. He didn't have time to process that before distant gunfire came. He'd take distant, even if it was right outside, to anything in his immediate vicinity. "Is that a *shootout*? Rye? You're…smiling?"

And taking Jonas' hand, a second before the words "Law enforcement!" in first English then Spanish came in a distorted voice. Through a megaphone, Jonas guessed, trying to piece together the sound collage. The door being blown off its hinges? A team entering the building? He would have peeked, but his eyes were screwed shut so tightly he didn't think he'd be able to ever open them again.

"Not reinforcements. Cavalry!" he yelled. "I bet they got the location because of those bastards livestreaming!"

"And the tracker in my boot heel," Rye agreed, squeezing Jonas' hand. Jonas squeezed back. Rye used his other hand to make a slight gap in the barricade for them to watch a stream of uniformed men pour in to fan out, the powerful lights they had with them bathing everything in a strong white glare.

Jonas shaded his eyes, wishing he could block out all the chaos as well as the brightness. He shook like a leaf and rammed a hand over his mouth to stop himself hurling. He felt like he'd just finished a marathon. Was this an adrenaline crash? He didn't know how much more he could take...certainly not the footsteps running toward his and Rye's hideout, the crash of it being dismantled and voices, all speaking at once, ordering them to surrender their weapons and lie on the ground.

"Stand down, men," drawled a voice, the accent similar to Rye's.

Jonas opened one eye.

"We have a brother Ranger in the house," the voice continued.

Jonas opened both eyes, in time to see Rye leap to his feet and clasp the man's hand.

That seemed to be a signal for general hand shaking and shoulder and back slapping all round, with different sets of uniformed men, including the DEA. Jonas shook all on his own, more like jello than a leaf now.

"Lieutenant LeGrande." Rye helped Jonas to his feet and held him. "You came through for me. This is Jonas Abrams, who I named in my case report. Jonas, Lieutenant LeGrande, our HQ lieutenant, and this is my senior captain, Chief Fischer, and...I don't see Assistant Chief Pereira?"

The two men Rye had named looked at each other then him and shook their heads, their expressions those of disgust and contempt. *Pereira, whoever he is, is in on it,* Jonas surmised.

"We had no idea..." The lieutenant seemed too choked to go on. "If we had, things would have been different, I assure you, Ryland."

"Well, we're cleaning house now," Fischer said. "And you'll play a big part in that, Ryland."

Of course. Rye would be the hero of the hour. Jonas nodded.

"There's a guard dog. Big Doberman, name of Pablo. Make sure he's okay?" Rye asked a guy with a walkie-talkie, who nodded.

"You doing okay there, son?" the lieutenant asked Jonas.

"I..." *Have no way to answer that.* "Do you know how Darrell's doing? Sergeant Darrell Williams? He was attacked. He's in hospital."

"Get on to it," Lieutenant LeGrande ordered a uniformed officer. "Any more questions?"

"I thought it was one riot, one Ranger?" Jonas replied, his voice as shaky as the rest of him. If Rye wasn't holding him, he'd have collapsed in a heap. He still might.

LeGrande gave a bark of a laugh. "Not when there's a Ranger in danger, son. Even one who thinks he doesn't need anyone, that he's fine by himself." He slapped Rye's upper arm and walked away in response to a shout.

Yeah. Rye did think that...just as Jonas did. And now things were over, and they had their lives to get back to. Jonas' head dropped on his shoulders.

"Jonas." Rye bent to get into his eyeline. "What you thinking there?"

"It's over?" Jonas asked. He *was* thinking a variation on that theme. "I mean, this is over?"

A uniformed officer, overhearing, laughed at that. "Speaks a civilian who'd never filled in paperwork," he said to a colleague, who chuckled.

"The case," Jonas tried to clarify. "They know you did nothing wrong. That you tried your best to get to the truth."

"I reckon." Rye shrugged.

"And you'll be back at work? At your real work, I mean. Not some made-up busy work at a kitschy museum?"

Rye frowned. "Jonas," he began, only to be cut off by a medic bustling over.

"Stand aside, sir," he asked Rye, shaking out the fold-up chair he carried in one hand and nodding at Jonas to sit on it.

Jonas had almost forgotten about his injuries but remembered and felt the pain of each one now he had to detail them, in chronological order while the medical officer noted then down on a chart and treated them.

"So you sustained no head injury and didn't lose consciousness. Good. Any nausea?" the medic asked, and Jonas shook his head, trying not to flinch at the pen light the man shone in his eyes to assess his pupil response. "And any feeling of faintness?"

"I wanted to throw up and being unconscious sounds good, but no," Jonas replied.

Smiling, the medical officer examined the rope marks on his wrists and smeared a sharp-smelling ointment on them that brought tears to Jonas' eyes.

"Can I go?" Jonas wanted to be anywhere but there.

"They'll be ready to take your statement soon. After that, probably," the medical officer told him, packing up his bag and walking away.

"Finally!" Rye burst out. "Come here." He kicked over a wooden crate to use as a seat and sat, beckoning Jonas over with his head. The intensity in his blue eyes had Jonas' heart thumping, and he sat before his knees collapsed under him.

"We got a lot to talk about," he started, and Jonas nodded. "What I said about y'all getting your rocks off fuckin' blue-collar guys who ain't your equals—"

Jonas blinked. "I wasn't expecting you to say that," he admitted. "But you did say that. And I do that."

"I understand why. I think. You gotta dominate. You don't in real life, so..."

"Like I *think* I understand why you like to submit. In real life you shoulder so much." Jonas shrugged. He was no psychologist. "It doesn't actually sound all that healthy."

"'S'fuckin' fun though." Rye grinned. "But yeah, I do carry on like—"

"The Lone Ranger?" Jonas said on a fake cough, all innocence.

"I'm used to it just being me. My sister and I, we lost our parents too young. I stepped up. And stayed there, just me, and maybe my attitude's wrong-headed. What you said, about me living for work...maybe that's true too. But if you love someone—"

"Someone...?" Jonas prompted.

"And wanna be with them," Rye continued, "you gotta look at how you live and carry on and fix stuff, you know?"

Jonas did know, and he wanted to. "Let bygones be bygones," he murmured, thinking of all the past he ought to let go of. "Do you believe in love at first sight?" he had to ask.

"I...don't know," Rye admitted.

"Neither do I," Jonas confessed. "It was more like fuck at first sight, anyway."

"God yeah." Rye nodded. "And I reckon that was enough of a start, right? Gave us something to build on?"

Jonas nodded back. They had.

"And my job, it's...important." Rye waved a hand, trying to explain. "But it ain't everything. Oh, y'all know what I'm tryin' to say! I don't got your fancy words."

"I got five fancy words for you," Jonas said. "They're an order, actually." He counted them off on his fingers as he said them. "Shut up and kiss me."

Rye did, and Jonas kissed back, pushing his tongue deep to dominate Rye's mouth, until the polite warning cough of someone approaching drew them apart.

"Our lives...they're so very different." Jonas looked at the uniformed law enforcement teams hurrying about. "Different careers, jobs, hours...and we live in different places. How will we make things work?"

Rye drew a finger down Jonas' nose. "We find a middle ground," he replied, his words a promise.

Chapter Twenty-One

"Anyone else's ass sore?" Jonas' voice asked, and Rye, straining to hear, caught a couple of yesses and grunts in reply.

Rye smiled. In the month that had passed since the showdown with the cartel, his ass was frequently sore after sex with Jonas. Right now, it was still feeling the effects of the vibrator Jonas had had him take early this morning, the biggest toy they'd used so far, which had stretched him *good*.

His balls still ached too, from Jonas edging him then denying him more times than they ever had so far, just as his dick still throbbed after the force and duration of the orgasm Jonas had finally permitted him. *Jesus Christ*, Rye had thought he was never gonna stop coming. Had anyone heard him yelling? His throat had been sore after, and he'd gotten looks at breakfast.

Now, he looked up from the campfire he'd built, where he was seeing to the meal, that he'd gone on ahead to their destination to get ready. He pushed his hat farther back on his head to regard the group of horseback riders arriving then thought of his words of a couple of weeks ago. He wanted to belly-laugh at how he'd persuaded Jonas that this place constituted part of the middle ground they'd discussed.

"You city slickers achin' and sore? And the river trail's the easy one," he commented.

"I'll say." Drew kicked both feet out of his stirrups and dismounted, English-style. "It's all very easy, with a saddle horn." He sniffed.

"Are you still going on about that?" Elliot took the hand Drew offered to get down from his ranch horse. "Well, if we have another Intrinsic Value vacation trip like this one, why don't we take it in England, and you demonstrate British horsemanship?"

"Ooh, could we go to Scotland?" Aldric, reaching them, begged. "You know I want to see men—"

"In kilts?" Drew joked.

"Drew!" Elliot reproved.

"Dance around swords!" Aldric, already a little red from being out in the Texas Hill Country sun, flushed deeper. "But anyway, this had to be an easy ride, for Darrell."

He went to help him down, but Lee, one of the Heartland Ranch owners, was there first, making sure Darrell, who'd thankfully almost fully recovered, got his feet on the ground safely.

"And even if it was a beginner trail, it was still amazing," Aldric continued, looking down to the lowlands they'd slowly climbed from to the flat crest of this hill with its cookout spot.

"'S'a good place," Lee agreed, swinging onto his pinto again. "I'm gonna go on, check the hill tops for erosion while I'm here." He pointed. "I'll be back in an hour or so to lead you home again. Want me to leave you a guard?"

"Yes, please," Rye replied at once.

Laughing, Lee, a former K-9 handler for the Texas Department of Public Safety, whistled, and a familiar black and tan Doberman walked up, leaving his scouting and escort duties to join his new owner. He listened to Lee's commands and, Rye thought, gave a small nod before letting Lee unclip his harness. Lee filled a plastic dish with water and told Pablo to drink. When the dog had drained it, he lay next to the fire. Lee tipped his hat and ambled off.

"I'm sure you only picked this place for our break so you could see how Pablo's doing," Jonas said.

"Looks to me like he's doing great here," Darrell replied. He took a seat, his back against a rock.

"Lee's a horse whisperer *and* a dog whisperer," Aldric whispered. "He's right. This is a good place. All the ex-service animals or, well, *difficult* ones, who find a home on this ranch are lucky to be here."

Rye nodded. He'd petitioned for Pablo to be given to the former DPS Trooper on his ranch.

"And now we're all lucky, because Rye is cooking," Jonas informed them.

"I'm not so good!" Rye protested. "I only do traditional stuff." Although he loved how much Jonas enjoyed and praised whatever he made.

"Well, it smells wonderful," Elliot said, sniffing at the campfire smoke that left gray plumes and spicy scent in the dry-grass and dust of the ranch.

"Yes — tish-oo!" Aldric's agreement after he took a deep sniff too turned into a sneeze. "Sorry. I really didn't know I was sensitive to — "

"Horsepitality," Drew said. He was still chuckling over that description, of what the Heartland Dude Ranch offered its guests.

"Until I got here. And yes, I took my antihistamine." He smiled before Darrell could fuss him about it, although from what Rye had seen, the fluffy-haired Aldric fussed over Darrell just as much. Just like Elliot and Drew looked out for each other. Like he and Jonas did.

Well, were starting to. Starting *out* to, really, in the month that had passed since that shit-awful scene in the old factory, where Jonas could have died. His cuts and bruises from being beaten had long faded, although he still had a scar on his arm from where the huge sliver of wood had cut it, but he occasionally woke at night from bad dreams about what had happened. Well, no wonder.

Rye made an effort to loosen his shoulders from where he tensed up whenever he thought about Jonas hurt or suffering, and accepted a kiss from Jonas instead, and his offer to help. "Yeah, you can take the corn off the heat and get everyone seated to eat it," he directed.

"And what about you?" Jonas asked, taking the tinfoil pack carefully.

"I gotta see to the Texas cheesesteaks first." Rye grinned. He had the steak and fixings mixed and it only took a minute to place the aluminum packet they were in onto the hot stones of the fire to cook through. He joined the group around the flat rock table that was sheltered by a half-circle of bigger rocks, ideal for leaning against, and passed out bottles of beer and soda. "Pablo, move around."

The dog did, making room and coming to Rye's side where he settled again.

"Oh, these are *good!*" Drew took another bite of his corn.

"Simple but good." Rye had queso with nachos ready for them next, in the skillet. He looked around the group. "I'm glad we could all do this." He wanted to get to know Jonas' friends. "Before you go to Europe, right?" he asked Drew and Elliot. Drew's Interpol work sounded glamorous, but Rye was a LEO and knew the adjective didn't belong in that world.

"France. Lyon," Drew replied, dabbing at his mouth to catch dripping butter from his corn. "It's not all cobbled streets and people riding bikes, like you're imagining, Aldric. It's a huge city."

"So it's just like San Antonio?" Aldric asked as he took a drink of soda.

"A bit, but more a university city than military." Drew laughed. "And funnily enough, so is Manchester, the UK base, where we're also going!" He took Elliot's hand.

"Where I'll be 'dead chuffed to have a brew'," Elliot said. "Drew's teaching me the language. He says that means 'very happy to have a cup of tea' but I won't say it until I'm sure." He gave a mock-suspicious look at his partner.

Rye nodded as he got up to stir the cheese and diced tomato-chili pepper mix into the sausage meat he had cooking. A former Scotland Yard detective, Drew now worked in the sharing of intelligence on security issues between public and private organizations within his sector. Anything that sought to reduce crime across the board was all right with Rye. He tipped the tortilla chips onto a metal plate and ladled the queso mix on top then sprinkled on the garnish.

"And Aldric's in charge of Intrinsic Value while Elliot's away." Jonas patted Aldric on his shoulder. "You'll do fine," he assured him.

"Yeah. Look how far you've come." Darrell held his soda bottle up in a toast. "You didn't think you'd cope with studying and now look at you, graduating community college with your associate degree! Everyone?"

They clinked bottles, making Aldric look embarrassed, but proud. "But I'm having a break before I go on to a bigger college for another two years to turn that into a bachelor's," he said.

He's gotta save up a little. Rye got it. "Well, dig in," he ordered the group, setting the communal plate down for people to scoop up the loaded nachos he'd made.

"Oh, wow!" Drew was again the first to help himself. "Tasty!" he said, muffled around a mouthful of cheese. "And hot!" He fanned his mouth when the cilantro and jalapeño topping bit.

"So you might both be studying at the same time!" Elliot remarked. "Or not? I don't even know if the written exam you'll be taking is one you study for, Darrell."

He'd applied to be a detective. "There's usually an investigator training program in your PD," Rye commented.

"Yeah, that's the case here," Darrell replied. "So I have to complete that and pass the exam once I have another six months' experience. Then I meet the requirements. My father thinks I should do it. He keeps asking me about it, prodding me, nudging me..."

He rolled his eyes as if it were embarrassing, but Rye knew from Jonas and from seeing a little himself that Darrell still couldn't believe his father had come around after spending years denigrating his middle son for having joined the SAPD instead of the military.

"He says he's coming to our five-a-side soccer ball team if Here's The Kicker get to the finals of the OutField league!" Aldric sounded like he could hardly believe it.

"He does know OutField is an LGBTQ sports association, doesn't he?" Drew asked.

Darrell smirked. "Guess he'll find out when he comes. But, Rye, you're gonna come back for that?"

"Sure will," Rye promised. "What, you reckon you got making the final in the bag?" He finished his share of the loaded chips as Darrell and Aldric dissected the competition, belittling the Bexar Bears, Ball Busters and Kick Me Baby One More Time.

"They don't even try!" Aldric scorned. Then his face dropped. "But you'll be gone."

Yeah, Rye was back in Waco full-time now, his reputation unsullied, with no need to return to San Antonio for any aspect of the case. Well, maybe for the trial, depending on where it was held.

"And Jonas will..." Aldric looked too sad to go on, and Darrell put his nacho down and took his hand.

"Honey, long-distance is hard," he said. "We should be glad Jonas will be with Rye."

"We'll miss you." Elliot looked teary-eyed too.

"Won't you miss teaching?" Drew asked. "I mean, you took a PhD and gave a good few years of your life to it."

"You're a born teacher." Aldric added his opinion. "I've had enough of them recently to know! You were so patient helping me learn all about the different antiques in the shop. The way you explained made things clear."

"And your love of history is so strong," Elliot said.

"Maybe... I did miss it and go back to it before," Jonas answered. "I could maybe pick up some hours or get cover work at Franklin or Baylor there, like I did at Laurel Heights here, or perhaps start at one of the two community colleges in Waco." He shrugged. "But for now, I'm taking a sabbatical...because I want to write!"

"Oh?" Elliot spoke, but he was by far the only one to look intrigued. "Somehow, I don't think you mean a history textbook?"

"No, I mean Wild West historical westerns, with a Texas Ranger hero!" Jonas' words almost tripped over one another as he explained what had been swirling around inside his head, taking shape slowly, since he'd been involved with the loan items for the museum exhibition.

Rye took the empty plate and checked the steak mixture he'd had cooking. *Yep, done.* He tipped spoonfuls onto huge bread buns, topping them with provolone. If it didn't melt right, like it would under a broiler, too bad. He piled the sandwiches onto the plate and set it down for the group to help themselves then retook his place, nodding when Jonas described the Rangers as being part of the history and mythology of the Old West.

"I didn't realize the early Texas Rangers were so multicultural," Drew said. "They really had Irish, Scottish and English men serving in their ranks?"

"Native Americans and Hispanics too, from privates to captains. The Bowie knives they used were made in Sheffield, England!" Jonas replied.

Jonas had learned this through the Ranger diaries and the company records that Rye had brought from the Waco Hall of Fame and Museum and Rye agreed with him that his idea of writing about such a group, albeit fictional, was a good one. Not all bygones were bad things to cling to.

"So Rye's your hero!" Aldric exclaimed.

"And Jonas is mine," Rye replied, pulling him close in a one-armed hug. How could he not be? The latest thing Rye was proud of about him was that Jonas was having therapy, to help him process all he'd been through, both recently and the stuff that had made him leave Dallas for San Antonio. He was an inspiration to Rye...who was considering counseling himself. *Finally.*

"Tell us the story you're writing," Aldric begged, so Jonas laid out more of his ideas, only stopping when Pablo got to his feet.

"Does that mean Lee's coming and it's time to head back?" Elliott groaned as he looked at their horses.

"Hey, it's a trick roping demonstration before dinner tonight, and after it's cowboy bingo," Drew reminded him. "Can't miss those!"

Elliott grunted as he stood. "Well, we'll sleep well tonight after all this fresh air."

The look Jonas shot Rye told him that he wouldn't be doing that much sleeping, and the grin Rye flashed at Jonas said Rye was more than good with that. With anything Jonas wanted to do to him. His cock twitched at the thought. He turned away to pack up and to conceal it.

"Aldric, what?" Darrell nudged him when he stood still. "You okay?"

"Oh, yes. I'm just thinking about us." Aldric's gesture meant the group.

"In what way?" Elliot asked. Jonas was curious too.

"About how three men working in an antiques store found their partners. Our strange and wonderful stories." Aldric looked around the six of them. "Someone should write about us!"

Want to see more from this author?
Here's a taster for you to enjoy!

Fire & Flutter:
Griffin Days and Pixie Nights
Bailey Bradford

Excerpt

"Sir!" The guard on duty outside the two-room suite in the Griffin Guardians HQ sprang to attention at Captain Gage's approach. He snapped out a smart salute, but his hand fell when Gage didn't march past but instead stood waiting in the corridor. "Sir...?" he repeated, uncertainly.

"As you were." Gage jerked his head to one side, illustrating how he wanted the corporal—returned to his position in between the doors and not in front of one of them.

The guard took a quick glance at the sheet of parchment paper pinned to the board on the wall. "Captain, you're not listed as—"

"Stand aside, *Corporal*." Gage added a raised eyebrow to the emphasis he placed on the last word and the junior officer recoiled.

Some officers might have raised their voice, or tapped their uniform badges, drawing the corporal's attention to the greater number of feathers displayed. That would have reminded the junior who was of a higher rank in the Griffin Guardians, the kingdom's elite federal law enforcement agency that griffin shifters ran and dedicated their lives to.

Gage never wanted or needed to pull rank, either here inside the HQ or outside. His height and breadth, coupled with his implacable, unflinching manner did it for him. Now was no different—the corporal not only scuttled to one side, but opened the door for him and saluted again. Gage murmured his thanks. While he liked how the junior officer had assessed and regrouped, he didn't like that a situation demanding such a response existed.

The list displayed outside in the corridor was a symbol of all that was going the wrong way in the Guardians, in Gage's opinion. This bureaucratic keeping account of which griffin shifter was assigned to which aspect of which case in which room at which time was getting out of claw.

What had Colm said last week? "*Pretty soon admin will be assigning us times for bathroom breaks, and probably make us sign in and out of the stall if we take a dump.*" It had been a joke, but Gage hadn't laughed. Not many of them had.

The two first lieutenants on duty in the observation room sprang to their feet, shooting puzzled looks at each other when Gage marched in, but both sat when Gage waved them down.

"Don't worry. I'm not here to supervise how you're implementing some new directive that came into force five minutes ago or check if you're reaching your latest performance targets," he told them, trying to sound lighter than he felt.

He made straight for the mirror-pane that divided this small room from the equally small but brighter room beyond.

It was a light-mirror, meaning that he couldn't use it to see his reflection, but he wasn't there to do that. He knew his uniform would be clean and crisp — Guardians' uniforms were designed that way — just as his blond hair, short back and sides and longer on top, was regulation length and cut. He bet his face bore the same narrow-eyed, focused look it always did. What he wanted was to look through the light-mirror to its other side.

But what he didn't expect was that the moment his gaze found the prisoner in the interrogation room, the prisoner would raise his head and stare back at him through the glass.

"The hells?" First Lieutenant Antonin exclaimed. His chair scraped on the floor behind him as he joined Gage. "He can't see through the glass?"

"He's a *mage*," Gage reminded his fellow officers, spitting the words out. "Who knows what these magic users can do?" His revulsion left a sour taste in his mouth as he continued, "His powers have been dampened, yes?"

"As much as the regs allow, Sir." First Lieutenant Sandrine joined them at the mirror, giving a choked-off exclamation when the prisoner sent a mocking finger-wave her way.

Gage swore. "This tricky bastard needs neutralizing, stat."

"I'm afraid we can't, Sir. Not until the request's been approved and stamped by two duty officers and the prisoner's been examined and cleared by the HQ physician." Antonin tucked his chair back into the table.

"New regulations, Sir," Sandrine added.

Both Antonin and Sandrine sounded apologetic, but it wasn't their fault, nor were they telling Gage anything he didn't know. Neither of those things made the information easier to hear, or the situation any easier to bear, however. Gage's hand had formed into a fist, and he exhaled as he opened it flat again, wishing he could huff away all the irritation and frustration he was feeling as easily.

Few people could say, their hand on their heart, that they loved their job, and Gage would never say that either, because being a Griffin Guardian was more than a job to him. The corps was his life, and he took pride in the knowledge that he'd given the organization his all since joining the Guardians thirty years ago. *That's good…isn't it? Laudable?* Because lately he'd begun to feel that, well, perhaps it wasn't.

He hauled in those stray thoughts. If he was feeling that there could perhaps be more to his life, it was because every moon-cycle seemed to bring with it new guidelines and directives, most of them aimed at giving what Gage still thought of as the lesser beings 'representation' or 'a voice' and making sure the higher beings — sorry, winged beings — didn't abuse what was becoming increasingly seen as their position of privilege.

Gage wasn't political or even very aware of interspecies politics. All he knew was that the new social climate made it increasingly hard for him to perform his duties, thanks to the 'accountability' and 'visibility' and every other hells-be-damned 'ility' the Equality Awareness Office dreamed up, and hamstrung the entire corps with, from its five-feathered general down to its lowliest private.

"Rules are one thing," he muttered. He liked rules. Lived by rules. Wished all the species did, that they followed the same ones as the griffin kingdom did. The griffins' codes of conduct and honor were revered throughout the plane, as was their ability to impose order, making them the natural choice for a federal law enforcement species. *A mission undertaken is a mission accomplished.* It was no coincidence that this was the Guardians' motto. "Rules keep things safe."

"I'm so sorry about Captain Colm, Sir," Sandrine said, perhaps catching Gage's last words.

Gage gave her a brusque nod in acknowledgment. He was sorry too. He'd had Colm as partner for the last ten years of his three decades in the Griffin Guardians, and they worked together well. Colm was as reliable and committed to getting the job done as Gage could want. There were always risks, in the job they did, of course, but to think that that contemptuous bastard sitting there —

"It was an accident. And I have no idea why he was chasing me. Why either of them were, these winged shifter beasts, whatever they were. Dragons, right?"

The mage's voice held defiance and there was triumph in the gaze he leveled at Gage through the glass as he spoke. But when he added a derisive kiss to the end of his sentence, Gage was out of the observation room and into the one next door almost before he was aware of moving or that he'd had all he could take. He had an assignment and he would do what it took to see it through. That was the way he operated. How he saw the world.

"Out," he ordered the second lieutenant in the interrogation room before the officer had gotten out the *S* of *Sir*. "Now!" he snapped. He rounded on the prisoner the second the door was closed, his eyes narrowed. "So. It's just you and me now, scum."

"I'm a *mage*," the prisoner snarked. "Which means that I'm —"

"Oh, excuse me. *Mage* scum," Gage snapped. "A mage scum con artist who used his 'magic' to rob money-vaults and businesses, having found a way around the thief protections. One who I came to question, which, for the record, is why you tried to run, and in your escape, you injured my partner." He let the fury he felt show.

"What? I did that? Well, that was wrong of me. I made a mistake there." The mage looked down at the desk in front of him for a few seconds. When he looked up again, his eyes grew darker as he turned his head slowly toward Gage. By the time he stared full force at him, his eyes were completely black, with no white to them at all. The effect was unnerving and the revealed strength of his powers worrying. Gage braced himself.

"Because I was aiming for the both of you." The mage got to his feet, his movements swift and jerky. Snakelike, almost. "You're stronger than your partner, though. Colm, wasn't it? Or isn't it, if he's still alive? Pity. A two-for-one hit-and-destroy would have saved me time and effort."

"Like you've saved us time and effort?" Gage kept his voice quiet when he wanted to yell at this piece of troll shit. "By confessing?" He smirked.

"Oh, if only anyone had witnessed it, either visually or audibly." The mage pulled a pitying face. "If only the mirror-glass hadn't silvered, and the listening holes hadn't all blocked." He gave Gage time to take in his meaning.

What – ? Gage took his eyes off the prisoner to throw a glance at the light-mirror and the conduit holes below it.

"Because without a record of this, it's like I was never here, griffin. And that being the case, I think I'll be off." The mage moved.

Instantly, Gage took a step forward to block him. "Oh, we just let you walk out of here, do we?" he scoffed.

The mage shrugged, as if he didn't care, then brought his hands up at lightning speed and weaved his fingers in a quick, complex pattern. "A state of balance or a lack of motion," he began, his voice low, and his eyes glowing a molten silver. Before Gage understood or could make him cease, he continued, his volume getting louder with each word, "A slowing or stoppage of a *flow*."

He brought his hands together on the last word, the clap loud, and the stasis spell he'd cast hit Gage like a punch to the stomach. It didn't have him staggering backward or knock him onto his ass like a physical blow would, though. Instead, it trapped him in place, unable to move. With a caw of triumph, the prisoner thumbed his nose at Gage, opened the door and walked out.

No. No no no! We should have neutered him, regulations be damned! Gage heaved in a breath, fighting with all his strength. That troll-dung mage had said Gage was stronger than his partner, which was true, but not true enough. Gage was stronger than any Griffin Guardian currently in the corps or in its records. He trained and honed the strength and resistance in his muscles and sinews and mind and spirit, increasing year-on-year what he could battle — and defeat.

Fighting the spell cast on him was like pulling himself along a too-narrow corridor whose walls were lined with broken glass, but he ignored the jagged shards ripping into him and actually — he saw, glancing down — rending his uniform and cutting his flesh. The pain barely registered and any spots of blood staining the gray tunic and pants vanished, just as rips in the fabric disappeared.

With one final almighty heave Gage was free. Panting, he shook off the remains of the stasis bind to hurl himself to the door. The mage was at the end of the corridor by now, and there was enough of his residual power left dusted on Gage for Gage to see the outline of the shield spell the prisoner had cloaked himself in.

The pull of the magic used snapped from its victim to its caster, the rogue mage who stopped in his tracks and turned around. The drop of the prisoner's jaw on seeing Gage free was the only amusing thing about the situation. The mage whipped around again and broke into a run.

"Stop!" Gage yelled, and the command in his voice had everyone freezing…everyone except the one he wanted to, the one who was making for the large window at the end of the corridor.

The mage ran faster, gathering speed and power. If that didn't give a hint about his escape plan, the hissed incantation and his hand outstretched toward the window did. A crack and the glass was gone. It hadn't shattered, but vanished, leaving the window frame gaping empty. The mage had already demonstrated an affinity with glass, but Gage had no intention of letting the bastard use it as an exit route. He sped up too.

"Captain, you can't!" Second Lieutenant Ralnd yelled behind him.

Oh, but Gage could. This was his case and he was doing whatever it took to close it.

Whatever it took.

About the Author

A native Texan, Bailey spends her days spinning stories around in her head, which has contributed to more than one incident of tripping over her own feet. Evenings are reserved for pounding away at the keyboard, as are early morning hours. Sleep? Doesn't happen much. Writing is too much fun, and there are too many characters bouncing about, tapping on Bailey's brain demanding to be let out.

Caffeine and chocolate are permanent fixtures in Bailey's office and are never far from hand at any given time. Removing either of those necessities from Bailey's presence can result in what is known as A Very, Very Scary Bailey and is not advised under any circumstances.

Bailey loves to hear from readers. You can find her contact information, website details and author profile page at https://www.pride-publishing.com

PUBLISHING

Sign up for our newsletter and find out about all our romance book releases, eBook sales and promotions, sneak peeks and FREE romance books!